Cowboy Vet
PAMELA BRITTON

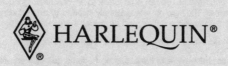

HARLEQUIN®

TORONTO • NEW YORK • LONDON
AMSTERDAM • PARIS • SYDNEY • HAMBURG
STOCKHOLM • ATHENS • TOKYO • MILAN • MADRID
PRAGUE • WARSAW • BUDAPEST • AUCKLAND

ISBN-13: 978-0-373-75147-1
ISBN-10: 0-373-75147-8

COWBOY VET

This edition published by arrangement with Harlequin Books S.A.

® and TM are trademarks of the publisher. Trademarks indicated with ® are registered in the United States Patent and Trademark Office, the Canadian Trade Marks Office and in other countries.

www.eHarlequin.com

Printed in U.S.A.

Dear Reader,

When I was in my teens, my friends and I had a *huge* crush on the large-animal vet who used to work on our horses. We would tease one another about calling the vet when our horses "sneezed" (actually just horse snorts) or when our horses needed their annual vaccinations (why couldn't we vaccinate them more frequently?). When that vet's truck pulled into the stable yard, we'd get as giddy as schoolgirls. Actually, I think we really *were* schoolgirls.

My hero in *Cowboy Vet* is nothing like the object of my childhood affection. (Okay, so my nose just grew a few inches.) Rand Sheppard is a culmination of all the vets who've worked on my horses over the years—yes, even the female veterinarians. To me, there's nothing more heroic than the men and women who stay up late at night tending to sick animals. This book is a tribute to each and every one of them.

I hope you enjoy *Cowboy Vet*. If you're in the mood to chat, feel free to drop me a line at www.pamelabritton.com. I love hearing from readers.

Pamela Britton

ABOUT THE AUTHOR

Pamela Britton never inflicted her early, unpublished works on friends or family. Instead she passed her books to the wives of famous race-car drivers and crew chiefs. Fortunately, the response was overwhelmingly positive, so she took the plunge and submitted them. Seven publishing contracts later, Pamela's work has been voted the best of the best by Barnes & Noble, the *Detroit Free Press* and *Romantic Times BOOKclub*. Recently one of Pamela's novels, *Scandal*, outsold J. K. Rowling—for two whole days.

You can visit Pamela on her wacky Web site, www.pamelabritton.com, or snail-mail her c/o P.O. Box 1281, Anderson, CA 96007.

This one's for all the real-life veterinarians
out there who've helped me with my animals
over the years. You're all the best.

Books by Pamela Britton

HARLEQUIN AMERICAN ROMANCE
 985—COWBOY LESSONS
1040—COWBOY TROUBLE
1122—COWBOY M.D.

HQN BOOKS
DANGEROUS CURVES
IN THE GROOVE

Chapter One

"Well, well, well. If it isn't Jessie the Jezebel."

Jessie Monroe stared down at the man who'd spoken, a row of windows to the right perfectly illuminating his handsome, scowling face. The glass coffeepot she held tipped dangerously toward his lap.

"Well, well, well," she mimicked. Her least favorite customer. "If it isn't Dr. Dolittle."

The restaurant seemed to grow quiet around them, everyone in the tiny diner no doubt listening in. Not surprising, since everyone supposedly "knew" what it was she'd "done" to Dr. Dolittle's cousin.

Dr. Sheppard leaned back, the orange vinyl squeaking in a way that sounded crass. He didn't seem to notice. "You going to pour me that cup of coffee or do I have to get it myself?"

She shifted her weight to her other leg, slowly lowering the pot, the liquid glug-glug-glugging as she poured. "Guess that answers your question, huh, Doc?"

"Guess it does." He gave her a smile that could only be called smug as he peered at her from beneath his black cowboy hat.

"I'll be back in a minute to take your order," she said in a monotone, turning away from his booth without giving him another glance. Damn the man. Not only did he think he was God's gift to women, but he always, *always* took pleasure in baiting her. His own form of revenge, she supposed.

"You and Dr. Cutie are exchanging evil glances again, I see," Mavis said, her dark skin glistening beneath one of the warming lights as she picked up four plates of food and balanced them precariously up her arms. It was late spring, but you wouldn't know it. The diner didn't have air-conditioning.

Jessie looked over at the table. "I think he likes me about as much as I like him."

"Well, then, I guess it's a good thing you don't have a crush on him like half the women in this town."

"Guess so," Jessie said. In fact, she was probably the *only* woman who didn't fancy the good doctor.

Not that she didn't understand his allure. She might not like him, but she was honest enough to admit that something in his eyes made her want to squirm.

Tall, dark and handsome he was, the term cliché and yet somehow appropriate. He looked like he belonged out on the range with a few hundred head of cattle milling nearby. There was nothing, absolutely nothing guaranteed to melt female hearts faster than a man who wore boots and who doctored furry little animals for a living.

"You gonna go back over and take his order, or shall I?" Mavis asked.

Jessie smiled. Leave it to Mavis to try to run interference. The two of them had formed a fast friendship the first day Jessie had come to work at the diner. They'd bonded over their mutual dislike of the pink polyester dresses they were forced to wear.

"No thanks, Mavis. I can handle Rand Sheppard."

"Can you?" the man himself asked when she walked up to him a second later, order book in hand.

Jessie turned as red as the blinking Open sign, or at least it felt that way.

Damn it, she hadn't meant him to hear. Or maybe she had. Her feelings always ran hot and cold where *he* was concerned. All that smirking self-confidence drove her nuts.

"Dr. Sheppard, I hate to bruise that overlarge ego of yours, but I've eaten men like you for breakfast."

"Yeah," he said softly. "So I've heard." He looked back at his menu. "I'll take the Rancher's Special with a side of bacon and English muffins."

"English muffins?" she said with a lift of her eyebrows. "Would you like some Earl Grey with that?"

"Nope. Just the muffins," he answered gruffly, back to his usual surly self.

"Coming right up." She tucked her pencil behind her ear, much easier to do ever since she'd chopped off all her red hair. "Rancher's Special with a side of bacon and English muffins," Jessie called out, slipping the order sheet into the spinner, then flicking it toward Frank. "Extra arsenic," she muttered under her breath.

But as she moved about the Kleenex box-shaped diner, she couldn't stop herself from glancing in Rand Sheppard's direction. It seemed every unmarried woman in town had set her cap for him—and failed to win him. And while Jessie knew better than to form a crush on the man, a part of her still wished he'd treat *her* as kindly as he treated everybody else. But that would never happen, she thought, watching as a man from the

Diamond W slid into the booth across from Rand. Jessie had one of the worst reputations in town, one that had started when she'd—supposedly— ruined Rand's cousin's life.

"She only lasted two days," she heard Rand say, over the clinking of dishes and silverware. "Shortest vet tech career at Sheppard Veterinary."

Vet tech? He'd hired a new vet tech? What had happened to Sandy Anders, his old one? The woman was an icon at Sheppard Veterinary, almost as much a fixture as the ancient wagon wheels that guarded the clinic's gate.

"So what are you going to do?" she heard the wrangler—Pete, she thought his name was—ask. Jessie picked up a hot plate while straining to listen. "You need help."

"I know," Rand answered.

She set the plate down in front of Hank, the smell of cooked bell peppers and cheese wafting up to her.

"Can I have some salt?" Hank was one of her regulars, a crusty old cowboy with a beat-up straw hat.

Jessie handed him the sugar.

"I said salt, Jessie." He tapped the scarred white laminate turned yellow with age.

She blinked. "Oh, yeah. Sure, Hank. Salt. Sorry."

She grabbed one of the forty salt-and-pepper sets on the bar beside the old-fashioned pie display, all the while listening in.

"You going to run another ad?" Pete asked.

"Guess I'll have to. But I don't hold out much hope of finding someone soon. You know how it is. Five hundred people want to work with animals, but only a few are qualified. Then they find out we're out in the sticks and, well…"

They didn't want to commute from the city. Jessie knew how it was. For three years she'd done the opposite commute from Los Molinos to the city— the nearby Bay Area. It'd taken her three years of night school and days of working in the diner, but she'd gotten her degree in animal science.

What Rand Sheppard didn't know was that she, Jessie the Jezebel, was a certified veterinary technician.

And she was about to ask Rand Sheppard for a job.

FIFTEEN MINUTES AFTER Pete had left, Rand didn't know what surprised him more, how hot the damn coffee was that Jessie Monroe served him, or that she slid into his booth after pouring him a cup.

"Mmph," he mumbled, as some of the coffee dribbled back onto his chin.

"Too hot, I know," she said.

And, as always happened when he looked at Jessie Monroe, he was struck by her eyes. Huge. And green, so green they looked like the new leaves that sprouted up around town. So green he found himself wondering yet again how the heck they could be such an impossible color. And then, as he always did when he caught himself staring, he remembered who she was.

"You could have told me it was hot," he said, whipping the paper napkin off his place mat, the silverware tinkling as it spilled onto the Formica table.

"Why warn you? You've eaten here enough times to know it's hot, and that it doesn't taste very good."

He did. And that irritated him all the more. She riled him. She always had—even before she'd been responsible for his cousin going to jail.

"Look," she said, peeking over her shoulder toward the kitchen where Frank flipped bacon, oblivious to his employee's defection, "I need to talk to you."

Rand leaned back, his hand crumpling the napkin beneath the table. His whole body tensed, although truth be told he'd been on edge ever since he'd seen who his server was.

"What about?" he asked, his fingers digging into the paper.

"I want to work for you."

If she'd told him she was about to rip her clothes off and dance naked, he couldn't have been more surprised. "What?" he asked.

Actually, he might *like* that....

"I want to interview for your vet tech job," she said, glancing at Frank again, the pink dress she wore gaping open as she leaned forward.

"But you're not qualified," he protested. Good Lord, the thought of Jessie Monroe coming to work for him...

"Actually," she said, lifting her chin, "I am. I have a degree in animal science."

What? "How?"

"Lots of late hours at the coffee shop while commuting to the Bay Area."

"Which college?"

"Gavilan," she said.

Something in his eyes must have made her think he wasn't impressed, because she added, "It's one of the top junior colleges in the state."

"I know it is," he said. It wasn't the college she'd gone to, it was that she wanted to work as his veterinary assistant. Her. Jessie Monroe. Who as a wild-child teenager had let Tommy take the rap for her.

Rand absolutely would *not* hire her.

"Look, Jessie," he said, "I've had hundreds of applicants—"

"Qualified applicants?" she asked, having obviously overheard him talking to Pete.

Rand tipped his head. "Some, yeah. My point being that there are people who've applied already, people I need to consider ahead of you."

"But I might be better qualified than them," she said. Her eyes seemed to shimmer. "Something you won't know unless you interview me."

"Nah. I've already looked over the applicants. A few of them have actual work experience, Jessie, not a bunch of college credits and a few lab classes under their belt."

"How do you know that's all I've got?"

"Educated guess."

She leaned toward him. "Sometimes the most highly educated individuals are incompetent."

"You got more than that?"

"Actually, I do," she said proudly. "I've been interning at a breeding farm in the Bay Area part-time."

"Then why don't you go work for them?"

"Because the commute is killing me."

He looked up at her. He didn't really believe that excuse. "Then move to the Bay Area."

"I don't want to move. I like this town."

"Jessie—"

"You just don't want to hire me," she interrupted.

"No. That's not it—"

"Bull," she said, slipping out of the booth. "Your refusal to interview me has nothing to do with my qualifications and everything to do with your cousin."

"Well, yeah," Rand said. "I'm not going to lie to you."

She stared, and he could have sworn he saw hurt in her eyes. "You still think those drugs were mine?"

"With your reputation, why would I think that?"

"Because people are innocent until proven guilty."

"There was nothing innocent about you."

"And Tommy Lockford, cousin to the great Rand Sheppard, was a saint."

"More of a saint than you were." Rand took another sip of coffee, even though the topic of conversation all but turned his stomach.

"So you think."

"So I know," he said, throwing her words back in her face.

She shook her head, her bangs falling in her eyes. She pushed them away impatiently. "Why did I think you might give me a shot?" she muttered under her breath. "You wouldn't hire me if I held a degree in veterinary medicine from UC Davis."

All right. Time to cut to the chase. "You're correct," he admitted. "I wouldn't."

She stiffened.

"Order up!" Frank called.

Jessie half turned toward her boss, then looked back again. "We're not through with this conversation, Dr. Sheppard."

"Yes, we are," he said in an equally stern tone. "You're too late. I've already got someone in mind."

She flicked her hair over her ears, her face coloring in a way that told him she knew he was lying.

"But if it looks like she's not going to work out, I'll let you know."

"No, you won't," she said, walking away.

And he wouldn't, Rand knew, because the idea of staring into those green eyes every day...well, it didn't bear thinking about.

When he paid his bill a short while later, he realized why he was so worked up.

He didn't want to hire Jessie because he had the hots for her.

And *that* was God's honest truth.

Chapter Two

He hated her.

It was undisputable fact, Jessie thought as she finished her shift, Dr. Sheppard having long since hit the road.

By the end of the week, Jessie wished she could give herself a frontal lobotomy. Every time she recalled their conversation she went from burning mad to horribly embarrassed. She couldn't believe she'd asked him for a job.

But no matter how humiliating, she didn't regret it. She'd do anything to break into her chosen field.

Which was probably why she found herself listening in on yet another conversation in the lineup at the espresso shop on her way to work.

"Hear he's had a devil of a time keeping up with all the work."

"That's what happens when you're the only large-animal vet in a town of two thousand."

"Yeah," said the first guy.

The sound of a coffee grinder filled the air; the chocolate smell of the beans made Jessie's mouth water. If only Frank made coffee as good as this place. "I tried to get an appointment with him this morning but his receptionist said he was on his way into the clinic for an emergency surgery."

"Gonna have a hell of a time doing that without an assistant. Or did he find someone?"

"Not as far as I know."

Surgery? Jessie thought, placing her order a moment later. If he was supposed to do surgery he would need help. Unless he sent the animal out to another clinic. But hauling a sick animal might put too much stress on it, which meant he'd have to—

"You know what?" she said to the young woman making her drink, who raised her diamond-pierced eyebrow. "Scratch that order," she said. "I'll be back in a bit."

If the woman was mad at her for leaving, Jessie didn't stick around to find out. She brushed by the people waiting in line and all but ran from the place.

Outside felt more like late winter than May. Los

Molinos's downtown strip was empty except in front of the Elegant Bean, where all the action usually took place this time of morning. Jessie snuggled into her down jacket, the faux fur around the hood tickling her cheek. The car she drove, a Honda that had seen better days, sat at the end of a string of vehicles. She was ten feet away when she saw the pool of radioactive-green coolant on the asphalt.

"Oh, Gladys," she said, wincing and shaking her head. "Not today."

A stream of vapor trailed her to the clinic on the other side of town. By the time she arrived, the motor gurgled as if it were on its last legs—and it probably was. She ignored it, choosing to deal with her engine's lack of performance later, after she'd talked to Rand. *If* she talked to him.

That was a big if, she thought as she slipped out of her car into the cool morning air, her cheeks momentarily heated, saunalike, by condensation leaking from her radiator. On the glass door, the words Los Molinos Veterinary Clinic stood out in white letters. Her heart pounded like the horses that ran behind the low buildings.

Unfortunately, that same heart stopped the moment she saw who manned the front desk: Pauline

Patterson, her childhood nemesis. Her old school-
mate really should have outgrown her animosity
toward Jessie, but had never forgiven her for stealing the object of Pauline's affection back in the
seventh grade.

Oh, great.

"Can I help you?" she asked, her eyes narrowed as she stared up at Jessie. She still wore
her brown hair feathered back even though Jessie
was pretty certain that style hadn't been popular
since the seventies—long before either of them
had been born.

"Is Dr. Sheppard in?" Jessie asked, inwardly
wincing at the malice she saw in the woman's
expression. Jeez. What would she have to do?
Whip herself with rosary beads and wear a
crown of thistles?

"What do you need to see him about?"

"I swallowed a mouse and I need his help getting it out," Jessie said, shifting her purse to her
other shoulder. Like the rest of her wardrobe, it'd
seen better days. The faux leather bag was peeling
away from its cotton backing. She hid it under her
armpit. Not that it mattered. Pauline's eyes hadn't
left her own.

"Okay, seriously. I heard he was on his way

here with an emergency surgery. I wondered if he might need help."

"He's not available right now."

She hadn't asked if he was available, Jessie almost pointed out. "Is he prepping for surgery?"

"I'm not at liberty to say."

Did Jessie have to pull a gun on her? "Okay. Well, will you tell him I stopped by? And that I'm available to assist?"

"You?" Pauline asked, her fleshy arms coming to rest on her desk. "Available to assist?"

"Yes, me," Jessie said, holding on to her temper by a thread.

"Since when do you know anything about veterinary medicine?"

"Since I graduated with an A.A. in veterinary science."

Pauline huffed in a way that had nothing to do with laughter. "Let me guess," she said, "you got it over the Internet."

Okay, that did it. "Pauline," Jessie said softly, drawing on the psych class she'd been forced to take for college credits, "I really don't understand your animosity. But I wish we could bury the hatchet, especially since I'd like your help in convincing Dr. Sheppard to hire me."

Silence. "You want Dr. Sheppard to hire you?" From the expression on Pauline's face, it was as if Jessie had announced her intention to cure cancer using nothing more than nose drops.

"Why not?" Jessie said. "I'm local. I love animals. And I have a degree."

"Well, I'm sure Dr. Sheppard will be thrilled to hear all about your qualifications, but no amount of schooling can teach a person integrity."

If Jessie didn't leave now, she'd do something she might regret. "Just tell Dr. Sheppard I dropped by, 'kay?" she asked. "Can you do that?"

All she got in response was what might be an attempt at a smile.

Jessie shook her head, turned around—

And ran smack dab into Dr. Sheppard.

"Jessie Monroe."

"Hello, Rand," she said, clutching his arms at the same time he held her by the shoulders, his black hat knocked askew, his big hands warm even through her thick coat.

His expression, however, was cold. "What are you doing here?"

HE KNEW HE SOUNDED RUDE, but he was in too much of a hurry to care.

"I stopped in to see if you needed help with your surgery."

The surgery? How had she known...? It really didn't matter. He glanced at Pauline. "Did Dr. Franklin call?"

His receptionist shook her head, her face creased in a frown. "Sorry, Doctor. He's out of the office for the week."

"Well, did you ask if his assistant could come?"

"There's nobody."

Damn it. He'd been dreading this exact scenario. In vain he'd tried to get a qualified vet tech out here to help out. Failing that, he'd tried to get an out-of-area vet to be on call. Normally that wasn't a problem, but for some reason every vet within a sixty-mile radius was either already on call for another clinic or out of the office.

"Where's Brandy?"

"She's in the back, cleaning kennels."

"Get her out here. I'm going to need her help with a C-section."

"But—"

Rand didn't wait to hear her response. Brandy wasn't qualified, but she would do. God willing, there'd be no complications from surgery that might require another pair of skilled hands.

"Rand, wait," Jessie said, following him outside to the horse trailer hooked up to his black, one-ton truck. Valerie, the owner of the mare—a college-age kid Rand knew wouldn't be able to afford the coming vet bill—stared at him with wide eyes. The mare on the other end of the lead rope stood with her head down, her chestnut sides dark with sweat.

"I don't have time to wait," he said, signaling the mare's owner to follow. "I've got a foal to get out."

"I can help with that," Jessie stated, stepping up alongside him, her short red hair framing her face.

"Brandy can help," he said curtly. That was all he needed—Jessie to mess things up.

His vet clinic was set up like most—main office at the front, equine exam room behind that, with a surgical facility and medical barn out back. He slid open one side of the double doors between the office and the surgical room, flicking on a light. "Bring her in here."

"Dr. Sheppard," Valerie said, "You know I can't pay—"

"I know. Don't worry."

When his gaze drifted past the frightened girl, he saw Jessie trailing in their wake.

"Jessie. Really. I don't need your—"

"Stuff it," she said. "You've got no assistant. I'm it."

He didn't have the energy to fight her—or the time. He led Jessie and Valerie to the surgical room.

Things happened in a hurry. The mare's water had broken nearly an hour ago. That meant the foal might have been oxygen-deprived for nearly a half hour. Not good.

The first test of Jessie's skill came within minutes. "Can you do a prep for me?" he asked.

"Where are the clippers?"

"Third drawer on the right."

She nodded; he turned away, gathering the medication he'd need.

The sound of the clippers filled the room as Rand hung the IV set on the hook suspended above the mare's back. His needle primed, he turned, surprised to see Jessie swabbing the area around the mare's jugular she'd just clipped, the stringent smell of alcohol filling the room.

"Ready," she said, stepping back.

Brandy showed up then, slowly shuffling her feet. Rand concealed his displeasure. The girl was never in a hurry to go anywhere, which meant trouble in a vet clinic, where seconds might count. Frankly, he probably would have fired her if he wasn't so short-staffed. He'd have to talk to her about that. Again.

"Lead her up," he told Brandy, signaling for the mare's owner to step back.

Brandy tried, but the tired mare didn't want to move.

"G'yup there," Jessie said before he could. "Go on." She slapped the horse on the rump and clucked.

That did the trick. Rand quickly administered the valium. Within seconds the big chestnut's knees buckled, then she went down. It took both Jessie and Rand to hook the unconscious mare to the hoist that would move her into position on the padded operating table.

"That's it," he said, the tricky procedure accomplished in a matter of minutes. Precious minutes.

Damn.

"Brandy, get the—"

But Jessie was already one step ahead of him, searching through drawers and finding the mouth tube.

"Can I do anything?" Brandy asked, fiddling nervously with the end of her brown ponytail. He'd had her assist with other surgeries, but she was still so new that she approached each procedure with trepidation.

"Just stand there for now." He inserted a catheter in the mare's vein as Jessie handed him the ends of the IV set. When he was done with that, she hooked the mare to the respirator and vital-signs monitor near the horse's head.

Impressive.

It was all he had time to think before he was busy getting instruments ready for the next step.

"You might want to go outside," he told Valerie.

The young girl didn't need to be told twice. She knew what was coming and knew it wouldn't be pretty. The question was, how would Jessie take it?

"What about me?" Brandy asked.

"Stay here. I might need you."

The sound of the hair trimmer buzzed through the air again, Jessie prepping the surgical area without glancing up. His estimation of her skills rose with each swipe of the clippers. She didn't need to be told where he'd be cutting. She obviously knew. And she knew how big an area to clip, too.

"You've done this before," he said.

"Once or twice," she offered, grabbing the Beta-dine she'd pulled off the counter, liberally swathing the area.

The breeding farm, he surmised. So she really had worked for one.

"Ready?" Jessie said, stepping out of the way, the latex gloves he hadn't even seen her pull on covered with the yellow-brown solution.

"Ready," he said, removing his cowboy hat and slipping on his own gloves.

He made the first incision, then looked sideways at Jessie. She didn't flinch.

Good.

He took the next instrument from her hand. In a matter of minutes he'd reached the foal, the mare's steady vital signs a rhythmic beep-beep-beep in his ears.

"Almost there," he said, reaching his gloved hand into the quarter horse's distended abdomen.

"Ooh, gross," Brandy said.

Rand ignored her. "Damn breeders are growing them bigger and bigger," he said, feeling around for a leg. "The mares just aren't equipped for a baby bred from a sixteen-two-hand stallion. Seems like I'm doing more and more of these of late."

"Sixteen-two?" Jessie asked.

He nodded, tongue between his teeth as he reached farther inside. "And that's on the smaller end of the scale. I'm seeing seventeen-hand stallions advertised in the *Quarter Horse Journal.*"

"Jeez."

And then he had it, his hand closing around a miniature hoof. After a tug that seemed almost too infinitesimal to do much, the foal slipped from the mare's abdomen.

"There we go."

"Oh, wow," Brandy gasped, reflecting how Rand felt every single time he welcomed a foal into the world. But it was far too soon to know if this little guy would be sticking around.

"Here," Jessie said, handing him a scalpel, which he used to rip open the placenta.

"Not breathing," he said. "Damn it."

He stuck his finger up the tiny foal's nostril, cleaning it out and then blowing into it in the hopes that he could jump-start the baby's lungs.

One breath.

Two.

The foal's chest suddenly twitched.

"Holy cow," Brandy said when the newborn's eyes opened.

"Here," Jessie said, handing him a stethoscope. Rand checked the foal's gum color. Within seconds they'd turned a healthy shade of pink.

"So far so good," he said, clearing more of the placenta from around the animal and then grabbing the stethoscope.

He checked the baby's heart, then the lungs. Clear of liquid. The foal tried to sit up, its unused neck muscles straining.

"Well?" Jessie said, and for the first time he heard emotion in her voice.

"I think he'll be all right," Rand murmured. "Brandy, come on over here and wipe the little guy down while Jessie and I close up."

Chapter Three

She'd impressed him.

Jessie wanted to punch the air as she exited the post-op stall ahead of Dr. Sheppard. She didn't, but it was damn hard not to smile.

The smell of fresh pine shavings filled the air, the horizontal aluminum bars that allowed people to see into the stalls gleaming in the late-morning light. It was a state-of-the-art barn, complete with closed-circuit cameras, heaters and even giant fans for those days when the Los Molinos mercury rose too high.

"So," she said, leaning against the bars and staring at the mare and foal. The foal was trying hard to stay balanced on his new legs. "When do you want me to start?"

No answer.

"Well?" she asked, glancing at him, her euphoria at a job well done making her bold.

"Jessie," he said, lifting his hat and running a hand through his hair. "I appreciate your help today, but I'm still not going to hire you."

"You're kidding me," she said in disbelief. "For goodness' sake, Rand, you couldn't have done that surgery without me."

"That's not true," he said, crossing his arms. He stared down at her in that serious way of his. The expression always made her uncomfortable. "Brandy could have helped."

"And lost you valuable time. That girl doesn't know OB pullers from a lead rope."

"She doesn't need to know," he said. "I could have told her what was needed."

Jessie stared up at him. "Look," she said, placing her hands on her hips. His eyes darted downward.

She stiffened.

Had he just—?

Nah, she told herself. He hadn't just looked at her breasts. No way. Dr. Rand Sheppard wouldn't give her a second glance.

She pulled her shoulders back nonetheless, under the pretext of hooking her thumbs in her belt loops, her elbows bent so that her breasts strained against the white T-shirt she'd worn beneath her beat-up jacket.

He glanced down again, only this time his eyes narrowed and he frowned, his mouth a flat line. "Look at what?"

He *was* checking her out.

Jessie couldn't believe it. He wasn't happy about it, she could tell, but that's what he'd just done.

She pulled her shoulders back even more, thrusting a hip out for good measure. "Look," she said, making her voice softer, "I understand you don't like me." *But you like my breasts.* "Let's put that aside for a moment," she said rocking slightly. "You're in a bind."

"I could hire somebody tomorrow if I wanted to."

"Then why don't you?" she asked.

"Because they're not qualified. Everyone who's applied so far has no experience and minimal education."

"Which just proves my point...or the point I was about to make. Hire me until a qualified applicant comes along."

He glanced down. And there it was again: *the look.* The one he tried too hard to deny—sexual interest.

He found her attractive.

In-ter-resting.

"If you find someone tomorrow, I'll leave," she added. "But I'll stay as long as you need me."

"I still don't think—"

"Rand," she said, clutching his arm.

He acted as if she'd touched him with a twelve-gauge needle.

"Don't—" he pulled back "—touch me."

Her eyes widened in surprise.

After all these years. After all the surly expressions. All the barbed comments. All the sarcastic retorts. He found her attractive.

"Sor-ry," she said. She tried unsuccessfully to suppress a smile.

"I don't like to be touched," he muttered.

"That must play hell on your love life."

He didn't answer.

She bit back a laugh. "As I was about to say," she resumed, "I don't mind being temporary help. Heck, it'll give me experience I can put on my résumé. Or are you willing to put the lives of the animals at risk by having someone like Brandy assist while you're out on calls?"

His lips went tight.

She knew she had him then.

"I'll bow out of your clinic the minute you find a suitable replacement."

A horse neighed, the answering calls momentarily filling the barn. Rand turned away, staring down the long aisle.

"Fine," he said, glancing back to her. "But it'll just be temporary."

"Got it," she said, trying hard to conceal her delight. "Temporary. When do you want me to start?"

Again he looked pained. "Tomorrow."

"Why not today?"

He shook his head.

Probably he needed to get his wandering eyes under control.

"Call me if you need me," she said.

All he did was nod.

Dr. Sheppard found her attractive.

Miracles would never cease.

IT'D BEEN A MOMENT of insanity. An act of desperation brought on by a long night spent keeping a colicky horse alive, followed by the emergency C-section.

At least that's what he told himself the next

morning, because there was no other reason he'd invite Jessie to work for him.

It's just temporary, he told himself as he slipped into the warm clinic.

"Morning, Doctor," Pauline said, shooting him a jowly smile that never failed to make him smile back.

"Mornin', Pauline."

Rand flipped through the mail he'd forgotten yesterday, thanks to back-to-back emergency calls. He'd sunk into bed exhausted, and praying that nobody's horse would founder or get colic or need emergency sutures.

"You've got three small-animal appointments, two need shots and one has a foxtail down his ear—or so the owner thinks. The foxtail is coming in first thing," Pauline said, peering over the eye-level counter that surrounded her like a corral. "I've scheduled your large-animal clients for this afternoon."

"Thanks," Rand said, tapping the edges of the envelopes on the Formica counter where they kept the patient sign-in sheet on a clipboard.

"And Jessie Monroe is waiting for you in your office."

The look Pauline gave him suggested he'd invited her least favorite politician to join him.

"I didn't know what to do with her, so I put her in there."

"Thanks," he said again. He'd deal with the censure he saw in the receptionist's eyes later.

His office was at the corner of the main clinic. It was a comfortable room that he'd paneled with real oak. Various western-themed items hung on the wall, from the skull of a cow to the horns of a watusi. Pictures of cowboys rounding up cattle hung on three walls; the fourth wall had windows that overlooked the front parking lot.

Jessie sat in one of the leather armchairs, the deep rust of the tanned hide matching the streaks in her red hair. She shot up when she saw him.

"Sleep in?"

"No," he said tersely, although that's exactly what he'd done.

She smiled. He ignored her, flipping through the mail stacked on his desk.

"I wasn't sure what time I was supposed to be here this morning."

"When we open is fine."

"You haven't changed your mind, have you?"

He had, at least a hundred times. Seeing her in front of him only reinforced his misgivings.

"Haven't changed my mind," he said, setting

the mail down and moving behind his desk. He felt a lot better with something between them. "Not yet."

"What's that supposed to mean?" she asked.

"Just that you should remember you're here on a trial basis."

"Oh, I remember."

"Good, because I just got three résumés in today's mail. If any of them look promising I'll have Pauline arrange an interview."

"I wonder what the odds are of that happening," he thought he heard her mutter.

"Excuse me?"

"Nothing," she said, sitting up straighter. "So, then, since you're not going to run me off with a shotgun, what do you want me to do?" Her smile was a little too bright.

"I've got clients coming in this morning. I'll expect you to do the pre-exam. This afternoon we'll go out on a few calls. You'll ride along. In between, help Brandy clean the kennels and the stalls."

"Terrific," Jessie said with another gamine smile.

"You won't think it's terrific when you see some of the animals we're treating. Colitis is going around."

She winced. The bacterial disorder caused

horses about as much discomfort as it did humans, and it wasn't pretty.

"I'm sure Brandy will be happy to have your help."

"I'm sure she will," Jessie said.

"But our first order of business will be checking the mare and foal you helped deliver yesterday. I glanced in on them a few times last night and I'm concerned the foal isn't nursing properly."

She nodded. "Will do. Boss."

Rand narrowed his eyes. It was the damnedest thing. Every time he met her gaze he felt almost itchy.

It was a feeling that followed him all the way out of the clinic. Rand scratched at the back of his neck and wondered if he'd picked up poison oak from one of the animals he'd treated.

"I can look in on them on my own," she said, walking beside him. "You know, if you've got better things to do."

She was peering up at him, and he noticed she had freckles sprinkled across her petite nose and high cheeks. But it was her lips that caught his attention. Their fullness specifically.

"No," he said. "I want to check the foal's motor skills this morning."

She nodded and the two of them padded down the rubber-matted aisle. It was his favorite time of day, when all the horses were munching their food, their teeth grinding against the alfalfa a rhythmic sound accompanied by the rustling of hooves in shavings.

"You know, Rand," she said. "You're very lucky."

He glanced down at her and wondered if her hair was naturally that red or if she dyed it. "What do you mean?"

"You have all this," she said, splaying her arms. "Every morning."

"Yeah?"

"I would give anything to surround myself with horses."

Something about the way she said it made him stop. Some people came to horses late in life. Some people never came to them at all. Jessie had grown up in a trailer park on the outside of town—a single-wide her mom supposedly still occupied—far away from the world of tiny foals and fancy barns.

"Maybe one day you will," he said.

Jessie smiled wistfully. "Well, in the meantime, this will do," she said, dropping her arms. "Thank you for hiring me. Even if it's for a day"

"You're welcome," Rand said, wondering why he suddenly felt like a heel.

Chapter Four

Jessie watched him walk away.

They'd checked on the foal, who seemed to be doing marvelously. Rand hardly cracked a smile as he finished his exam. When he left he didn't even glance at her, just ordered her to help Brandy muck out stalls.

Jessie went to the groom stall he'd mentioned, finding a rake leaning in a corner and a wheelbarrow tipped upward so that the rim rested against the rubber-padded wall.

If he wanted her to clean stalls, she'd clean stalls. She'd be the best damn stall cleaner he'd ever seen.

So that's what she did, working through the morning and occasionally catching glimpses of Dr. Doom through the horizontal bars. She waited for him to call her in to help him with some of his small animals, but apparently, despite what he'd told her earlier about doing pre-exams, Brandy was his assistant of choice. That seemed silly. Brandy didn't know a thing, but Jessie supposed she shouldn't be surprised. She had a feeling Rand would give her a wide berth whenever possible.

Story of her life.

When it was time to go out with him on his afternoon calls, she'd been so busy all morning she was almost relieved at the prospect of sitting in his truck.

"We've got five calls to make," he said, the two of them stopping next to his one-ton. "While we're out with clients I'll expect you to gather my supplies, keep control of the horses and, if I don't need you for either of those two things, to stay out of my way."

"Yeah...okay," she said, all but sighing as her butt made contact with the seat. Jessie didn't feel his stare at first, and when she did, she lifted an eyebrow. "What?"

"If you're not up to this, Jessie, say the word and you can stay here at the clinic."

"What do you mean?"

"You look apprehensive."

"Not apprehensive, just tired," she said. "But don't worry, I'll catch my second wind in a minute."

"You sure?"

"Let's go," she urged, giving him a wide smile.

They set off, Jessie staring out at the rolling hills, the scenery speeding by, all the while wondering if she'd deluded herself when she'd leaped to the conclusion that Rand found her attractive. Today he appeared to have himself well in hand, his shoot-Jessie-down radar firmly in place.

But still, some little devil made her straighten up, made her turn her body toward him and ask, "So, Dr. Sheppard…dating anyone?"

He did a double take. "Who wants to know?"

Me, she wanted to say, but only because she thought it'd be hilarious to see his reaction. "Just curious," she said. "All the single women in town go gaga over you. I was wondering if one of them had caught your attention."

"And if one had?" he asked, scanning her with a quick flick of his eyes.

"I would offer her my sincerest condolences and then give her the business card of a good psychologist."

He sent her another quick glance, only this time his eyes were narrowed beneath his black hat. "You know, for someone already on shaky ground, you sure do like to mess with me."

"I try," she said.

They both lapsed into silence, which lasted until their first stop, a fancy ranch-style home—butter-yellow—with a prefab barn out back. A fresh-faced girl who didn't appear old enough to have lost her baby teeth came outside to greet them, her boots and riding pants proclaiming her to be of the hunter-jumper set, the expression on her face announcing her to be a bona fide member of the Gaga for Dr. Sheppard Club.

It was a beautiful facility, especially impressive considering it was privately owned. Jessie forced herself not to stop and admire the luxurious surroundings, but focus on why they were here. A horse stood on crossties in the middle of the aisle in the barn, a big gray with white dapples along his neck and body.

"Hey, Lacy," Rand said. "How you doing?"

"Fine," she said, "but I wish Mongo was better."

Forget the barn—and Rand—Mongo was gorgeous.

His head looked as sculpted as an Arabian's, his body thick with muscles. But his feet were huge. Platter-size, actually. Warm blood, she thought. A type of equine developed from draft horse stock that usually came in two sizes: large and extra large. And an extra, *extra* large price tag.

"I just don't know what could be wrong with him," his owner was saying. "He came back from the desert circuit fine. I even gave him a week off. But when I took him out this morning, he could barely walk."

Rand nodded, running his hand down the horse's legs and checking for elevated pulse points that might indicate lameness. He also checked for heat and swelling, his expression perplexed when he didn't appear to find anything.

"I don't see anything yet, Lacy. Hey, Jessie, get me the hoof testers."

She nodded and quickly fetched the tong-shaped instrument that reminded her of a fireplace tool, watching as he used it to apply pressure in various spots on each of the horse's hooves.

"Nothing so far," he said, straightening.

"Really?" Lacy asked.

"Really," he said. "But that doesn't mean he might not be injured higher up. Jessie, trot him out so we can see what happens."

"Maybe I should do that," Lacy said. "He's kind of a handful on the ground."

"No, no," Jessie said. "I can do it." She smiled at the woman.

"He sure has gotten big, Lacy," she heard Rand say, tipping his hat back to get a better look.

"I know. Do you remember when my mom and dad bought him? Best graduation present I could ever have gotten. I've won just about everything there is on him."

Graduation? The girl was old enough to have graduated from high school? And she'd gotten a twenty-thousand-dollar horse for a present? Maybe a forty-thousand-dollar horse. Must be nice.

But when Jessie asked the animal to walk forward, she forgot all about the price because it quickly became obvious that Mongo was indeed a handful. Actually, he was a terror, she thought when he tried to nip her arm.

"Careful," Rand said.

"Maybe I should do it," Lacy repeated.

Jessie shook her head. "No, no. It's okay. I can do it."

If she had to walk naked, up a cactus-infested hillside, barefoot, she'd do that before letting Mongo's owner do her job.

"Come on, Mongo," Jessie muttered, clucking her tongue against the roof of her mouth.

The gelding dug in his heels. She tugged harder.

It was like pulling against a tractor...or an oil derrick.

"Maybe I should—" interrupted the owner.

"No, no. I've handled animals his size before." *Oh, yeah? When?*

"Come on," she said again, flicking the excess lead rope behind her so that it slapped the gelding's belly.

He shot forward so fast she felt like a mouse tethered to a hot air balloon.

"Holy—" She cut off her curse because all at once she had to keep up with the beast, and to do that she had to run. For every three steps *she* took, the horse took one. Jessie was forced to half hop, half skip to keep up.

The distinctive clip-clop-clunk of a horse whose gait was off rang out. The animal's head bobbed every time his right front hoof hit the ground.

"Poor baby," she said, forgetting her animosity.

"Okay, that's far enough," Rand called.

"Whoa," Jessie ordered.

The horse kept going. Big surprise.

She planted her heels.

And he *still* kept going.

Her feet left furrows in the ground. She would have laughed, but she was too busy trying to stop the horse. Jessie called out a stern "Whoa" again before something embarrassing could happen, such as losing her footing.

But the horse, in the perverse way of equines, didn't want to whoa. Jessie could have sworn she saw the beast wrinkle his nose at her.

That did it.

She pulled on the rope with everything she had, giving herself rope burn in the process, and digging her feet into the ground as if she was anchoring the *Titanic*. And in a way, she was.

Mongo, likely stunned by the sudden dead weight, stopped.

"Good boy," she wheezed, out of breath. She resisted the urge to double over and gasp.

"Okay," she heard Rand call. Was that amusement in his voice? "Bring him back."

"Great," she muttered. "I was afraid he'd say that." And then she turned and peered up at the huge gray. "If you do that again, I'm calling Alpo."

The horse's head flicked up; his ears swiveled back and forth, back and forth.

"Yeah, that's right. Alpo. Or maybe Elmer's Glue. Or the restaurant down the street from where I live. Whatever. Just don't cross me."

She eyed the horse. He eyed her back. She then

slid the end of the braided cord through the gelding's halter, just below his chin, the rope serving as a makeshift chin strap. "Let's see how you like this," she said, taking a deep breath before setting off again.

He didn't want to trot, and she really didn't blame him. If her foot hurt, she wouldn't want to run, either. But she made him move by using the same technique as before—a flick of the rope—except this time she was prepared for his quick lunge forward. And this time when she asked him to stop, he obeyed, the pressure on his chin obviously doing the trick.

"Yup. Right front," Rand said as she halted, winded—but trying not to look it. And even though his eyes were shaded by his hat, she could see his amusement.

Miracle of miracles.

"Thought you were going for a ride there," he said.

"Me, too."

"You really think it's the right front?" Lacy asked. "I thought it was the left rear."

"Nope. It's the front. Jessie, we'll need to take X rays. Do you know how to do that?"

"Of course," she said.

"Good. Then hand Mongo off to Lacy and help me set up the equipment."

WHAT THE HELL WAS WRONG with him? Rand thought as he gathered the square X-ray plates. He was supposed to be checking a horse for soundness and all he could think about was how impressive Jessie had looked bravely trotting that big gelding back and forth.

And how a smile changed the color of her eyes.

"Here," he said, handing her the thick film.

"Hey!" She shifted quickly to avoid dropping the plates.

"Sorry," he muttered, turning to grab the portable machine, which resembled a tiny generator more than a piece of high-tech equipment.

"What's wrong?" Jessie asked, her head tipping sideways so that her red hair touched her shoulder.

He released a breath, easing his neck. She had every reason to stare at him that way. She was doing a good job—a *damn* good job—and he'd yet to commend her on it.

"Nothing's wrong," he said, scratching his neck again. Damn poison oak, or whatever it was. "You're doing a great job, Jessie," he admitted. "I thought for sure that horse was going to drag you all the way to the main road."

"Me, too," she confessed again, and there was that smile…

He used the brim of his hat to shield his eyes. "When I find someone for my clinic, you won't have to worry about getting a recommendation from me."

Then why don't you hire her?

"Really?" she asked.

Because I believe in self-preservation.

"Really."

"Oh, jeez, thanks. You have no idea how much easier it'll be for me to find a job with a recommendation from an actual vet, not one of my instructors, or the people I've been interning for."

The grin she gave him was open. Free.

Special.

"You're welcome," he said gruffly.

Lord, he better find somebody soon.

Very soon.

Chapter Five

Jessie didn't know what to do.

They worked well together, she realized. That should have surprised her, but it didn't. The simple truth was she had always had a secret crush on the good doctor. What woman in town hadn't? Even Mongo's owner, as young as she was, had flirted with him.

But it wasn't until they were on the last call of the day, Jessie and Rand having diagnosed five horses that afternoon, that she realized just how bad she had it.

After they left the last barn, Rand pulled over to fill up his big truck with diesel and then headed inside to pay. Jessie waited a minute then followed in his wake, the cool air ruffling her hair as she looked for the Ladies sign.

"She's gonna be gone in a matter of days, Phil."
Rand's voice brought her up short.

"Well, I don't like it. That girl is trouble with a capital T. Or have you forgotten what happened to Tommy?"

"I haven't forgotten anything," Rand said. "She's just a temp. That's all."

Jessie glanced at the clerk, who was staring at her, likely because she was standing half in and half out of the store and the bell was still ringing. She stepped all the way inside, glancing left. Rand, apparently so focused on his conversation that he hadn't noticed the dinging bell, stood near the soda case, his back to her, shoulder-high racks of chips shielding her from his view. She had to crane to the right to see who he was talking to, not that she didn't already know. Phil Lockford, Tommy's father.

Oh, brother.

She started to turn away, but Phil's next words made her pause. "She put my boy in jail," he said, his voice low and full of hostility. The man had never had that much hair, but it seemed thinner now, the color having turned gray. He had a long face and crooked nose, red—although from anger or drink, she didn't know. "You're my nephew. I can't believe you'd even let her in the building."

She pushed the door open again. She could wait to use the restroom.

"Believe me, Phil," she heard over her shoulder. "I don't want her around any more than you do."

Jessie stiffened.

"I'm thinking of letting her go when we get back to the clinic."

"Well, that's more like it." The rest of what he said was lost as she stepped blindly outside, nearly getting hit by a car worming its way among the parked cars and gas pumps.

I'm thinking of letting her go.

Damn it, the words hurt, more than she would have thought possible.

Did you expect Rand to defend you?

She jerked open the door of the truck. That's exactly what she'd been expecting, she realized, inhaling her anger. She'd been expecting him to tell Phil he was starting to believe the drugs in Tommy's glove compartment hadn't actually been hers. That she wasn't a screwup. That she deserved respect.

Instead he was going to fire her.

RAND CLIMBED INTO THE truck a few minutes later, orange drink in hand. Jessie had gotten herself under control by then, enough so that she wasn't shaking with rage. He didn't say anything as he started the engine, and that was okay with her. She was afraid if she opened her mouth she'd say something rude.

"Thanks for your help today," he said as he pulled to a stop in front of his clinic, in the parking spot reserved for him.

"You're welcome," she said, getting out fast.

She didn't wait for him to catch up, just pushed the glass door open in a way that more than likely startled Pauline. Jessie didn't care. She didn't even glance to see if her old pal was sitting at her station, although she assumed she was—could practically feel her venom. Jessie was going to collect her purse and then get the hell out of there.

Rand Sheppard could go to hell.

"Jessie, wait," he said as she went into the tiny kitchen that served as a break room.

"I'm in a hurry," she said, bending down and opening the cabinet where the women on staff stashed their purses. She couldn't believe it; there were tears in her eyes. Tears. She hadn't cried in years. Not since Tommy Lockford had so completely betrayed her by claiming *she* was the drug addict, not him. A lie that half the town had swallowed, thanks to her party-girl reputation and Tommy's spotless one.

"What's the matter?" Rand asked as she straightened, purse in hand.

"Why don't you ask Phil Lockford?"

He drew back, his big shoulders filling the doorway. "You heard that?"

"I heard enough," she said. "If you're going to let me go, just tell me right now."

Once again his cowboy hat left his eyes in shadow. Still, he stared at her with such intensity she felt immobilized.

"I don't really want to let you go."

She lifted her chin. "That's not how it sounded."

"I was just trying to placate Phil."

"And see," she said, "that's the problem. You didn't even *defend* me. I busted my rear today to help you out and you couldn't even say one word about that to Phil." Or that she might be innocent.

Rand was speechless for a second or two. She could see his Adam's apple bob. And then he looked away. "I don't want to let you go, Jessie, but you know I have to."

"Why?"

"You know why, and it has nothing to do with

your skills as a vet tech—or what happened between you and Tommy."

And then, to her shock, he touched her, his big hand turning her face up to his. "Let's not play games with each other."

Her heart began to thud as loudly as Mongo's hooves.

Rand's head lowered. She told herself not to let him do it. He shouldn't cross the line. It would be bad.

For her?

Or him?

And then their lips connected.

She'd often fantasized what it would be like to kiss Rand.

It was way better than a fantasy.

She felt his breath on her cheek, felt his lips, surprisingly soft.

Oh, jeez.

And then the kiss changed. It went from tentative to hungry in the matter of a heartbeat. Then they were gulping at each other, their mouths open and tongues touching in a way that made Jessie gasp. Perfect. He tasted so perfect.

She leaned toward him, needing contact with his tall body.

"Dr. Sheppard, your mom's on line two."

They broke apart. For half a heartbeat, Jessie thought the words had come from behind them. But they'd been disembodied, Pauline's voice coming from overhead—a speaker.

Rand stared down at Jessie for what seemed like an eternity, his chest rising and falling nearly as rapidly as her own. He turned toward the phone on the counter, pressed a button and said, "Tell her I'll be right there."

Not overhead, then, Jessie realized. Pauline's voice had come from the speakerphone. "Will do."

They faced each other. "That was stupid," Rand said.

"I know," she agreed, shocked at the regret she felt…and the disappointment.

"I'm sorry," he muttered.

"Now what do we do?"

"I don't think it'd be a good idea to work together."

No, she supposed not.

"I'll have a letter of recommendation typed up by tomorrow."

She nodded. So he was going to fire her. "Fine," she said softly. "Thanks for giving me a try."

"Good luck, Jessie."

Good luck, Jessie.

That was it? No *I'll give you a call?* No *Let's go to dinner?*

She stared up at him, waiting, and when he didn't say anything, she turned away. She should have known better. She might have impressed him with her job skills, but obviously she hadn't gained his respect.

RAND BOWED HIS HEAD the moment the door closed behind her.

"Damn it."

He flexed his tingling hand, shaking his head as he thought about the confusing mix of emotions Jessie raised in him.

She'd surprised him.

She hadn't propositioned him when she'd been fired. Hadn't begged for her job. Truth was, she'd looked as disappointed by the turn of events as he felt.

"Damn it," he said again.

"Doctor?" Pauline said, reminding him that he had a call.

He picked up the phone. "Yeah," he said into the receiver, realizing in an instant that he'd sounded curt. His mom would likely tear into him for that.

"Rand," she said, her voice completely devoid of emotion. "You better come quick. It's Peanut."

Chapter Six

The Diamond W was a half hour from town. That night, it seemed like the world's longest drive.

Rand found his mom out back behind the plantation-style house, in the ancient barn that had turned gunmetal-gray with age. She was inside Peanut's stall; the poor animal appeared the worse for wear.

"Any improvement?" Rand asked as he let himself in.

Martha Sheppard shook her head, a few strands of gray hair escaping from her bun. "It's not good, Rand," she said, her eyes on the pony. "I gave her the Bamamine like you suggested, but it hasn't helped. I've been having a hell of a time keeping her on her feet." The pony's snow-white sides were expanding and contracting rapidly, her rear leg poised to kick at her stomach. "But what has me panicked is the color of her gums."

Rand lifted the pony's lips, "Crap. She's impacted," he said, studying the purple shade. "Let's see if she's ruptured."

He missed Jessie's presence then, felt a brief moment of surprise at how quickly she'd come to mind. Damn it. He could use her help right now.

"Lead her on out," he said. "I'm going to need to shave her stomach."

But his mom knew the routine. Peanut was twenty-five years old, ancient by equine standards. They'd kept her healthy with a lot of TLC and luck, but lately she'd been colicky.

"Her gut sounds are normal," he said, "and her heart is pumping good and strong—no murmurs that might indicate the beginnings of system failure."

He made quick work of shaving the stomach area, then drew some fluid.

He got blood. That was all.

His face must have showed his relief, because his mother let out a shaky breath.

"Okay. So she's not ruptured, which means the obstruction must be pressing against an artery. If we can get the blockage to pass... Let's go ahead and tube her, but if she doesn't improve I'm going to have to take her to the clinic."

His mom nodded, her face pinched with worry. She had a special place in her heart for Peanut. She'd entrusted the little Shetland with her children's lives, and it was a trust that had never been broken. For that, Peanut had earned herself one of the biggest stalls on the ranch, oats every day and a life of luxury. A life Rand hoped would continue for a very long time.

Twenty minutes later he'd done everything he could. He'd inserted a tube through her nose and pumped oil into her stomach. He'd given her extra painkillers and something else to help her relax. All that was left to do was wait.

WAITING DIDN'T WORK.

By midnight, Rand knew it was bad. The pony's pulse had begun to elevate, her gums turning dark purple, almost black.

"I'm going to take her down to the clinic," he told his mom.

"You going to operate?" she asked, wiping a strand of hair off her cheek.

"I'm going to have to. It's too much of a risk."

She nodded, shrugging deeper into her bulky

jacket. She looked so vulnerable… Rand was reminded that his mom was getting up there in years. Of course, she hadn't been the same since his dad died.

Rand gave her a quick hug. "I'll go hook up the trailer."

He hoped they'd be able to get the pony loaded. She was pumped so full of medicine, it'd be difficult to get her to walk, much less step into a trailer.

They ended up having to just about lift her inside. He'd tied her head tight, hoping if the pain got too bad she wouldn't roll. He did one other thing, too.

He called Jessie.

"Who you dialing at this time of night?" his mom asked. The headlights of the truck lit the long driveway, making the shrubs resemble ink blots.

"Vet tech."

Even though it was dark inside the cab, he could see she appeared worried.

"Hello," said a sleepy voice on the other end of the phone.

"It's Rand."

"Rand," she said, his name coming out as a panicked yelp. "What's wrong? Is it the foal?"

"I have a colic surgery coming in."

"Be there in ten minutes."

That's all she said. No sarcastic comments. No "I'm in bed."

She continued to surprise him.

"I thought you hadn't hired anyone," his mom said, managing to sound both exhausted and puzzled.

"I haven't. Jessie's a temp."

"Jessie?"

He nodded.

"Certainly not Jessie Monroe."

"Mom, your cognitive abilities never cease to amaze me."

"I'm old, not brain dead."

"You're *not* old," he said.

"And you're changing the subject. What the heck are you doing with Jessie Monroe?"

"She's helping me out at the clinic," he admitted. "Turns out she's pretty good."

"I didn't even know she'd gone to college," his mom muttered.

"She has an A.A. degree. Earned it going to school at night."

"You sound almost proud of that."

He glanced at her and in the lights on his dash saw her frown. "She's good, Mom, and given how I used to think of her, that's saying a lot."

"*Used* to think of her?" Those blue eyes were still sharp.

"She's changed," he said. "For the better."

"Do you really think so?"

"I do." He remembered what it felt like to kiss her. Despite his concern for Peanut, his pulse rate speeded up.

"Maybe not."

SHE BEAT HIM to the clinic. Jessie waited outside, her car radiator releasing steam that rose like tiny cumulous clouds and disappeared into the night. Poor Gladys. The quick-fix fluid Jessie had poured into the thing must be breaking down. Darn it. She needed to get it repaired.

Headlights flashed across the front of the clinic. She turned, expecting to see Dr. Sheppard's truck. Instead she spied a fancy silver truck pulling an equally fancy horse trailer, with Diamond W painted in big, bold letters on the side.

Rand was driving. And there was someone in the truck with him.

His mom.

Jessie groaned. Her memories of the day Tommy Lockford had been tried and sent to jail were still vivid. Martha Sheppard had been at the courthouse—not surprising since Tommy was her nephew. Jessie would never forget the woman's fury when they'd come face-to-face. She hadn't raised her voice. She hadn't lifted a hand. All she'd done was tell Jessie exactly what she thought of her. And even though Jessie always tried to put a brave face on things, Martha had wounded her to the core. Not so much because of what she'd said, but because Martha Sheppard was a woman Jessie had always looked up to, and she'd actually *believed* Tommy's lies. That had hurt, especially when everyone in town had taken their cue from her.

An overhead light spilled cool white light over the gravel driveway. "Hey," she said when Rand got out. Jessie wrapped her arms around herself and tucked her hands beneath her elbows to keep them warm.

"Hey," he replied.

"What can I do?" she asked, glancing toward Martha. Nothing about her ever seemed to age. Her body was still just as plump. Her hair was still as silver, the white-blond of a palomino's mane. Her face was still unlined, except for thin crevices around her eyes. Odd, because Jessie had yet to see the woman smile.

"Go on in and unlock everything," he said, tossing her the keys.

Jessie glanced toward Martha again. The older woman ignored her, heading toward the back of the horse trailer.

"Okay," she said.

"Jessie." Rand gave her a look, one of kindness mixed with reassurance. "Thanks for coming."

"You're welcome."

She'd been shown the day before how to disarm the alarm, so she made quick work of opening doors and turning on lights. It was warmer inside, but not by much, the exam room's roll-up door affording marginal insulation against the late-night cold. When she opened it, the chain rattled like a funhouse sound effect. Rand and Martha were on the other side, a small white pony between them.

Jessie met Rand's gaze, startled. "This is Peanut," he said. "She taught all us boys how to ride."

He didn't need to say anything more. Jessie could see what the pony meant to him and his mother.

"What can I do to help?"

Chapter Seven

They'd had to operate.

Ultrasound and X-ray had revealed a massive obstruction in the pony's lower intestine. The surgery had taken an hour, but once Rand removed the blockage, the pony's color had immediately improved, giving them all hope that Peanut might recover.

Still, it was going to be a long night.

"You can go on home now," Rand told Jessie, clearly exhausted but never leaving the pony, who stood, head hanging, in the middle of the stall. Rubber mats and shavings covered the floor. Strapped to her neck, an IV pack slowly dripped sodium and a mix of antibiotics and painkillers into her system.

"I'm not going anywhere," Jessie said, glancing

at Rand's mom, who looked just as exhausted as her son. The woman hadn't said a word to her though the pre-op or surgery. "You're the one who needs rest. And you, Mrs. Sheppard. I've had some sleep, unlike the two of you."

"Are you saying I look like hell?" Martha asked.

Jessie straightened, shaking her head so that her short hair tickled her cheeks. "No. Of course not. I'm just saying the two of you appear exhausted. You've been up most of the night." She glanced inside the white-paneled stall. "Go get some rest. I can keep an eye on Peanut."

"Mom. Don't tease her," Rand said without looking up from the notes he was writing on the pony's chart. "She's not used to your acerbic sense of humor."

"Who says I'm teasing her?"

"And quit acting so hard-nosed. You're just as grateful for Jessie's help tonight as I am."

Jessie looked from mother to son, thinking Rand had to be mistaken.

"I am grateful," Martha said, and to Jessie's surprise, the words didn't sound the least bit grudging. "But I don't think she should be here alone. What if something happens?"

"I'll tell you what," Rand said, hanging the chart

on the outside of the stall, right next to the dry erase information chart. "Pauline will be here within the hour. I'll have her drive you home."

Jessie gasped. "The diner. I forgot I'm supposed to work this morning."

"I'll tell Frank you're working with me."

"That'll go over well," Jessie said, wrinkling her nose.

"It will if I tell him I'll vet his dogs for free."

Jessie raised her eyebrows. "You're right, that'll work."

"I don't need someone to drive me home," Martha said, hugging her well-worn jacket.

"You do, too," Rand argued. "I'm not letting you get behind the wheel after being up all night."

"Rand Sheppard, I've been a rancher's daughter my whole life. Lack of sleep isn't going to kill me."

"No, but it might make you fall asleep at the wheel. I'll have Pauline take you home."

"What about you? You need rest, too," Martha said.

"Are you kidding? This is old hat for me. I'm the only large-animal vet in town."

"It wouldn't be old hat if you did as I suggested and hired someone else to work with you."

"Mom—"

To Jessie's shock, Martha smiled in her direction. "He's as hard-headed as his dad used to be."

"I've noticed," Jessie said.

Martha's smile faded. Rand's dad had died only last year. Jessie watched as Martha glanced at the stall before holding out her hand. "Thank you for your help, Jessie."

"You're welcome, Mrs. Sheppard."

Mother and son turned away and Jessie realized that was the closest to an apology she would ever get out of the woman.

When Rand returned a short while later, Jessie had just checked Peanut's vitals.

"How's she doing?"

"Okay," Jessie said. "Temperature's a touch high, but that's to be expected after surgery."

"Any bowel sounds?"

"Not yet."

As they stared at each other she was reminded of their kiss.

"Did you get your mom off okay?" she asked, looking away from him. A rush of physical awareness had warmed her body, and Jessie worried he might see the evidence in her red cheeks.

"She went home. Reluctantly, and only after I promised I'd call her if anything changed."

"She sure loves that pony."

"We all love her," Rand said.

When Jessie got up the courage to look at him, he was staring into the stall. It was early morning, but it was hard to tell that inside the post-op barn. Fluorescent fixtures refracted light off the polished aluminum walls. Those same lights made his face look pallid, the skin beneath his eyes smudged black.

Her stomach did something odd then. And Jessie realized an instant later that she felt sorry for him.

"Are you okay?" she asked.

"Never bucked on me once," he said with a hint of a smile.

"I hear that's pretty rare. Most ponies can be little stink bombs."

He smiled. "Stink bombs. Yeah. That's a good way of putting it."

Her stomach was doing that fluttery thing again, only this time it had nothing to do with pity.

"What was it like?" she found herself asking. "What was it like to grow up on a ranch? To be surrounded by all that land?"

And all that love.

"It was the best childhood a boy could ask for."

She bet it had been.

"My older brother and I used to saddle up Peanut and ride her down to the lake. This poor pony made more trips than the local train. My mom would always know where to find us. Sometimes she'd even ride out herself and bring us lunch."

"It must have been wonderful."

He glanced over at Jessie, and appeared to consider what she'd said. "It was."

She pulled at some hay that had collected between the thick, vertical bars. "I didn't do it, you know."

"Do what?"

She took a deep breath, tried to calm herself then looked him square in the eye. "Those weren't my drugs in Tommy's car. They were his."

To her surprise, his expression didn't change. He didn't look at her in disbelief, didn't immediately dismiss her words with a flip comment, didn't do anything but stand there and wait—presumably to hear her side of the story.

"I know you probably don't believe me. I know it looked bad that my cousin ended up being your cousin's supplier, but I swear to you I had nothing to do with it."

Peanut lifted her head and tried to take a step toward her water.

"She's thirsty," Rand said.

"Should I give her some?"

"Two or three sips ought to do it. I'll check her gut."

Jessie nodded, but before she could slip by, he stepped in front of her.

It felt as if her heart stopped. She looked up slowly, her pulse resuming at a frantic rate.

"It's not that I don't believe you, Jessie," he said softly. "I just need time to think about it. Time to maybe readjust my thinking."

She nodded, suddenly sad.

Maybe readjust his thinking.

"I understand."

He looked as if he might say something else, but the sound of Peanut's hooves scraping across the rubber mat caught her attention. "I'll go get the water," she said.

Jessie felt like a fool. Obviously she was good enough to kiss, but not good enough to believe.

Chapter Eight

Martha didn't care what her son said; she didn't need half as much rest as he seemed to think. And when her horses were sick, she liked to check on them like she would her children. In some ways, they *were* her children.

She found Peanut right where she expected, still in the middle of the stall, still looking miserable. What she didn't expect to see was Jessie with her, lovingly stroking Peanut's neck, the battered, dark blue jacket she wore rustling as she moved her arm.

"You'll be all right," Jessie was saying as she tried to comb out the pony's mane with her hand. "Rand'll fix you all up. I promise."

Martha watched, curious, as Jessie scratched the pony right behind the withers, the sweet spot. Peanut lifted her head slightly, eyes half-closed.

But what held Martha rapt, what caused her not to announce her presence, was the look on Jessie's face. Her expression was so full of sympathetic understanding, her murmured "Poor thing" so heartfelt, Martha found herself studying her anew.

It was like looking at a distorted image in a mirror. It was the same Jessie—and yet *not*. There was no sign of the reckless teenager. There was maturity in her face, and strength, and weariness. She'd been up half the night. No wonder she looked tired. The younger Jessie wouldn't have stayed up late for anything but a party.

"Mom?"

Martha jumped. So did Jessie, the two of them catching each other's eye at the same moment before Martha glanced at her son. "You scared the devil out of me," she said, placing her hand on her chest for added effect.

"That I doubt," Rand said, giving her a wry look. "How's the pony?"

"I don't know," Martha stated. "I only just got here myself." Well, that was true. Sort of. "How's the pony, Jessie?"

"Improving," she said. "Vital signs are leveling off and her gut sounds are better."

Rand unclipped the chart from the front of the

stall, checking the notes someone had made—most likely Jessie. He nodded, tipping his hat back.

Martha glanced at Jessie, who looked away instantly. But not before Martha saw her face.

Jessie fancied Rand.

What's more, Martha was pretty certain Rand fancied Jessie right back.

Well, I'll be.

No wonder Rand had been quick to call Jessie. And no wonder she had been quick to come to his aid.

They *liked* each other.

But what had Martha catching her breath in surprise was the way *she* felt about the whole thing. Twenty-four hours ago she'd have pulled her son aside and warned him not to make a fool of himself. But that was before she'd watched Jessie help save Peanut's life.

That was before she realized *this* Jessie wasn't the same girl she remembered.

"Jessie's right," Rand said, studying the chart. "Her vital signs look good. No red flags. Her labs came back positive, too. No toxicity in her system. Course, I'll feel better when her temperature goes down and her vital signs have stabilized, but there's time for that."

Martha nodded. And as always happened when she heard Rand talk about his patients, she felt only pride. Her boys were everything to her, their baby sister, Caroline, every bit as special. Martha didn't know what she'd done to deserve such good kids, but her fondest wish was that they'd settle down and be happy—as she had with their dad. Nick, her oldest, had recently fallen in love.

Maybe it was Rand's turn.

But with Jessie Monroe?

It might take getting used to, but Martha could tell a lot about a person by the way he or she handled four-legged critters. The way Jessie touched animals spoke volumes.

"Mom," Rand said, "there really isn't any need for you to be down here. If something happens, I'll let you know."

"Don't be silly. I had a two-hour nap, which is probably more than you've had," she said, eyeing her son critically. "Jessie, have you had a break?" she asked, glancing back at the girl.

You'd have thought she'd asked if Jessie had given birth by the way she started.

"Uh, no. I haven't. But that's okay. I had rest earlier—"

"Then let's go get a cup of coffee," Martha said, waving her arm. "You look tired, too."

"But I think Rand—"

"He can spare you, can't you, Rand?"

It was hard to tell who looked more shocked, Jessie or her son. Martha bit back a chuckle.

"No. I don't mind at all," Rand said.

"Good." Martha opened the stall door. "Just let me give Peanut a quick hug goodbye and then we can be off."

COFFEE WITH MARTHA Sheppard.

Jessie felt like a prisoner about to sit down with the head warden.

"Mrs. Sheppard, really, there's no need to buy me a cup of coffee."

"Nonsense. And call me Martha."

Jessie felt her mouth start to drop open. She slammed it closed.

Martha had made a point of ignoring her the past few years. In fact, she'd been known to cross the street if she saw Jessie coming. Now, suddenly, she was inviting her to coffee.

Why?

They took Martha's car, a vintage Cadillac that looked as if it'd just been driven off the showroom floor. Jessie remembered when the Sheppards had gotten the car. They'd been the talk of the town. She couldn't believe Martha still had the thing. Years ago, whenever Jessie had seen her and the Sheppard kids drive around town, she'd wondered what it would be like to ride in such luxury.

And now here she was.

"You really shouldn't be such a slave to Rand, you know."

Jessie closed the door, marveling at how heavy it was. Her own car door felt like a piece of tin in comparison. "Oh, I'm not," she said, sliding onto the smooth leather seats. The vehicle was spotless inside.

"He doesn't like a woman who's too passive."

Okay, that comment gave Jessie pause. It almost sounded as if Martha was giving her tips on how to ensnare her son. She must really be tired. "Believe me," Jessie said, "I don't let him push me around."

"No?" Martha asked, starting the car. "That'll pique his interest. He's been spoiled by women his whole life, you know. First me and then his sister. Doesn't help that he's one of the most eligible bachelors in town."

Unreal. This was Rand they were talking about. Her *son*.

But then it dawned on Jessie. Suddenly she

understood why they were having this conversation, and she couldn't conceal the hurt.

She took a deep breath, then said, "You don't have to worry that I'll make a pass at your son, Mrs. Sheppard. I'm not interested in him that way."

They were moving toward the wrought-iron gate at the clinic entrance when Martha jammed on the brakes. "You're so full of shit, I'm surprised your eyes aren't brown."

Jessie lost the battle; her mouth dropped open.

"And that's not why I was saying that at all," Rand's mother stated.

"It's not?"

She shook her head. "You like him, don't you?"

Jessie thought about lying, thought about brushing the comment off in some glib way, but knew Martha would see right through her. She had that knack. "I've had a crush on him since tenth grade."

Martha rested her arm across the steering wheel. She wore a fleece jacket—beige with a pattern of brown horses running along the bottom edges. She might be close to seventy, but she was still stunningly beautiful. "You know," she said, "a lot of women fancy my son."

"Do you mind *me* fancying him?"

"I'm not sure."

"Mrs. Sheppard—"

"No, no. Let me finish. I'm not too puffed up with my own self-importance that I can't admit when I might have been wrong."

Jessie caught her breath, her body paralyzed by a rush of emotion. There was a look in Martha's eyes, one that made Jessie think—

"Watching you with Peanut, seeing you care for her... You've changed."

"I *have* changed," Jessie said.

Martha looked at her with such intensity it was as if she were reading the thoughts in Jessie's head. "I know."

Jessie's eyes began to burn. She felt moisture build around the rim of her lashes. After all these years... "It means a lot to me that you can see that."

"Were those your drugs in Tommy's glove compartment?"

Jessie was momentarily struck dumb by the question, then emphatically shook her head.

Martha stared at her for another long second. "Humph. Well, what's in the past is in the past."

Jessie's eyes were suddenly awash in tears. She just wished Martha's son was as easily convinced.

"If you want Rand, Jessie, I suggest you go after him."

"Wh-what?"

"You heard me. Nobody ever got anywhere in life by sitting on their behind. You seem to understand that, Jessie. I'm just surprised you haven't applied that lesson to your personal life."

And with that, she gave her a wide smile and hit the accelerator.

Chapter Nine

By that afternoon, Peanut had started to recover. She still had a temperature, which Rand expected to last for the next couple of days, but her temperament had improved and she wanted to eat.

Jessie returned with his mom, both of them breaking into smiles when he told them the news.

"So you think she's going to be okay?" Martha asked.

"It's looking good so far."

"Thank god," his mom said, her hand at her chest.

"So you can go on home now," Rand said. "Unless you want to take Jessie to an early dinner now. Or maybe shopping," he added. It was strange that his mom would change her attitude toward Jessie, but in actuality not all that surprising. That was the way she was. She either liked you or she didn't. No in-between.

"No, no," Martha said, shooting Jessie a glance. "She needs to be here."

Rand looked from one woman to the other, tilting his head. What was that look the two of them had just exchanged?

"I don't know if Rand wants me around," Jessie said. "I'm not officially an employee, you know."

"And why is that?" Martha asked. "She's good, Rand. You should hire her."

"Maybe Jessie doesn't want to work for me," he said, studying her face for any sign that she remembered why they'd decided it was a bad idea.

She blushed.

Oh, yeah, she remembered.

"It's not an easy job, Mom."

"Jessie, you want to work here?"

Jessie looked as if she was stuck between a rock and a hard place. "Well, I—"

"There, you see? She does. I'd take her up on the offer, Rand. You'd be hard-pressed to find someone better."

Wow. That was a stamp of approval if ever he'd heard one. The question was, what was responsible for the abrupt change of heart?

And had his mom *really* just maneuvered him

into rehiring Jessie Monroe? "Well?" he asked, holding his breath.

"Rand, I—"

"I really could use the help."

"Maybe we could do that temporary thing again," she said.

"Sounds good to me."

"Just so I have something on my résumé," she added.

"That makes sense."

No, it didn't. None of it made sense. And yet here they stood.

"You'll be working some weekends, too," he said.

"More kennels?" she asked.

"And stalls."

"Aah, now I know why you want me back," she said with a smile.

"Just so we understand each other."

"Well," his mom said, "now that that's settled, I'm going to say goodbye to Peanut again, but I'll be back later."

"Maybe we can have dinner," Rand suggested, determined to get to the bottom of her sudden change of heart.

"That'd be nice." She stretched up to kiss him

on the cheek. "I remember when you were the one to get on tiptoe to kiss me."

"I remember, too," he said softly.

She gave his arm a squeeze. "Thanks for saving Peanut's life."

"We're not out of the woods yet."

"But I know between you and Jessie she's in good hands."

She nodded at Jessie, the two of them exchanging another private look Rand was hard-pressed to understand, and then went inside.

"She's nice," Jessie said into the silence.

"She's a handful." He shook his head. It felt as if he was standing inside a box that had just been overturned. "But she's right," he admitted. "You're good, Jessie. I don't think I need to tell you how much help you were to me today. And I promise what happened in the break room won't happen again."

"It won't?"

"It won't," he affirmed.

She lifted her chin, smirking. "Then I guess I have nothing to worry about."

"I wanted to reassure you, because I have a rodeo to work this weekend."

"Rodeo?"

"I'm the attending animal physician," he explained.

"I didn't know rodeos had such a thing."

"They do, and I always bring my assistant along."

"I see."

"We'll just be driving down together," he said. "Rodeo management provides the hotel rooms. We'll be back late Sunday."

"Who covers the clinic while you're gone?"

"It varies. Sometimes nobody, but that's rare. I always try to get a qualified vet in here to handle emergencies."

"And how long will we be gone?"

"Just a couple of days. You can drive down separately if you like."

He could tell she was thinking it over. "No," she finally said. "We can go together."

He gulped—he couldn't help it. And he wouldn't be surprised if Jessie had heard him. Judging by her expression, he thought she probably had.

"Great," he said. "We'll need to leave by one."

"No problem."

Unfortunately, Rand had a feeling it *would* be a problem.

THEY LEFT FOR THE RODEO the next afternoon. Rand had told her to meet him at the clinic, so Jessie showed up with her purse slung over her shoulder and an overnight bag in hand.

It was a big truck, a diesel with a back seat about as big as the front, so there was plenty of room for her legs. Behind the F-350 he pulled a stock trailer. Sunlight shone off the rig's polished aluminum surface like it would off a mirror. She had to squint when she glanced at him, and was just in time to see him shift away from her.

"Why the trailer?"

"Sometimes I haul stock for friends. A friend of mine asked me to bring a couple of bulls to the rodeo."

That explained the mooing in the back. "How long is the drive?" she asked.

"We'll be there in less than an hour."

She nodded.

"I don't like to be too far away from home," he said, his eyes taking in her outfit. It was the new shirt she'd bought with last week's tip money that caught Dr. Sheppard's attention— not surprising, since the scooped neckline exposed a lot of flesh.

"Is there something wrong with my shirt?" she asked when he glanced at her yet again.

"Not if you're trying to attract every cowboy at the rodeo."

"I *beg* your pardon," she said, indignation making her sit up straighter. All right, indignation mixed with humor.

"Only buckle bunnies wear that kind of stuff."

"What stuff?" she asked innocently.

"When you bend down I can see just about all the way to your navel."

"You cannot," she scoffed.

"Yes, I can. When you got in I caught a glimpse of your bra."

"What were you doing looking at my bra?"

"It…it was an accident."

She laughed; she couldn't help it. He sounded so petulant. Like a kid who'd just hit a baseball through a window."

"What's so funny?" he asked.

"You," she answered, shaking her head and looking out the window. They hadn't even left the clinic yet, Rand having forgotten to start the truck.

"What about me?"

She looked back at him, still smiling. "You can't keep your eyes off me."

He stiffened as if she'd poked him in the ribs. For a second she thought he might deny it, or that he might say something derogatory about her shirt again. Instead he said, "Dressed like that, what do you expect?"

"It's just jeans and a top, Dr. Sheppard," she said. "Granted, it's not one of those button-up, western tops cowgirls are known to wear, but it's perfectly acceptable rodeo attire."

"Not for my assistant."

"You're just jealous I didn't dress this way for you," she felt emboldened to say.

"And you're playing with fire," he said softly, his eyes dark beneath the cowboy hat. She felt the heat in that gaze cross her body like the caress of a warm hand.

"I know," she admitted.

He looked straight ahead, tipping his hat up before starting the truck. "If you're testing my resolve, you've picked a hell of a time to do it."

"Why's that?"

He put the truck in gear, backing out of his spot. "Because tonight we're sharing a hotel room."

Chapter Ten

He was just joking, but it was a joke that backfired.

Because the look in her eyes made him think things he had no business thinking.

"Really?" she asked.

"No."

Rand told himself to look away. The electricity in the cab made him feel as if his nerve endings had misfired.

"Chicken," she said softly.

He released a breath. Put the truck in Drive. They lapsed into silence for the rest of the ride, Rand's thoughts spinning.

She was flirting with him. *Flirting.*

And damned if he didn't want to flirt back.

He decided to try and ignore her. But that proved impossible. She smelled like...vanilla. The damn scent seemed to permeate the entire cab. And that sexy shirt of hers…it pulled taut over her breasts, offering just a hint of cleavage and making him wonder what it'd be like to lift it up, to taste the flesh beneath—

Stop it.

She was his assistant, and right now he didn't want to lose another one. But more importantly, this was Jessie Monroe, and even though she'd proved herself professionally, she had yet to prove herself to him personally.

They arrived one long, torturous hour later, Rand pulling his rig to a stop behind the chutes. He couldn't get out of the truck fast enough. The temperature difference between the Santa Cruz mountains and Los Molinos became evident immediately. The Hamilton Hills Rodeo Grounds were nestled in the foothills that separated the Bay Area from the coast. Trees of every shape and size surrounded the arena, mostly tall pines and thick oaks. On clear days those trees would provide shade for the contestants, but today all they did was make it hard to see the practice arena. It was overcast, too, the clouds so thick they seemed to hang down from the sky, causing beads of moisture to instantly form on the brim of his hat and the shoulders of the dark green jacket he pulled on.

"You're going to freeze," he said to Jessie.

"It smells good," she stated, inhaling deeply, her breasts rising as she did so.

And he wondered if she was talking about him or the rodeo grounds.

He had to take a deep breath himself before he could squeeze any words out. "There's an extra jacket in the back. Help yourself."

"What else is back there?" she asked, raising an eyebrow.

He stuffed his hands in his pockets. "Jessie—"

"Well, I'll be," someone interrupted. "It's Rand Sheppard."

"Chase Cavenaugh," Rand said, glad for the interruption. "Long time no see."

"That's for sure," his longtime friend said. The man had been one of the best damn bull riders in the business before he'd chucked it all to become a stock contractor. "Where you been?"

"Here and there," Rand said. "You supplying stock for this gig?"

"Just the horses. And it's nice to know they'll be in good hands should one of them get injured. Your sister riding?"

"Nah," Rand said. "This is too small-time for her now. Caro's off doing some rodeo in Utah."

"You think she'll make it to the National Finals Rodeo?"

"If she doesn't make it and win the whole shebang, I'd be stunned." Rand turned to Jessie. "Chase, you know Jessie, don't you?"

To his surprise, Chase's face lit up. "Jessie Monroe. What the heck are you doing here?"

"Hey, Chase," she said, sinking into the man's arms. "Lani let you out for the weekend?"

Chase tipped his hat back and stared into Jessie's upturned face. "Actually, she's here, but just for tonight, and she'll be disappointed to know our kids' favorite babysitter won't be around this weekend—or will you be going home tonight?

'No, I'm here for the weekend."

"I think she wanted to go out to dinner with Amanda Berrigner. One of those girls' night out things."

Jessie smiled and then shook her head. "I'm afraid my babysitting days are over. Or haven't you heard I'm Dr. Sheppard's new assistant?"

Chase stepped back, his eyebrows raised. "You got the job?"

"I did."

"Well, good for you. I always knew you'd land on your feet."

Rand looked back and forth between the two of them, his gut twitching at the expression on her face. It was a moment or two before he identified how he felt.

Jealous.

He was jealous of Chase, which was about as stupid as trying to catch a bull by the tail. Chase was married. Had been for five years now, quite happily. His wife, Lani, was about the sweetest and funniest women Rand had met. Chase wouldn't cheat on her. And Jessie wouldn't make a play for him. Rand knew that much about her by now.

"How are the kids?" Jessie asked.

"Well, Rose is gonna do mutton busting tonight," Chase said. "She's addicted to it. Ever since she got on her first sheep at the Little Britches Rodeo she's been pestering us to let her do it again."

"So you decided to bring her along," Jessie said.

"Are you kidding? It's the reason why I agreed to do this rodeo. No mutton busting, no deal. At least that's what Rose told me to tell the promoter."

Jessie laughed. "I can just hear her saying that."

"You know my daughter well."

"And if she's anything like her dad, she's probably pretty good at mutton busting."

"That she is," Chase said, his voice filled with pride. "Lani says she's going to ride bulls with the boys one day." He glanced at Rand, laughing. "I tell her over my dead body."

"I'm gonna go check in with Rob," Rand said.

Chase lifted a hand, the two of them hardly noticing his departure. Rand heard Jessie laugh again at something Chase said, and his stomach churned.

What the hell was going on? Chase was a married man. If there was anybody on this earth he should trust with Jessie, it was Chase.

Rand stopped. Anybody he'd *trust* with Jessie? Why the hell did he need to *trust* someone with her? Jessie wasn't his girlfriend. Trust wasn't an issue.

He glanced back.

Or was it?

"WHAT'S UP WITH YOU and Rand?" Chase asked.

Rand's jaw was so tense she could see it from where they stood. "He has the hots for me and doesn't want to admit it."

"Rand Sheppard?" Chase asked incredulously, cocking his straw cowboy hat. "Are you sure?"

Jessie wrapped her arms around herself for

warmth. Her shirt might be cute, but it wasn't exactly practical. "Positive," she said, glad to spill the beans to someone. She'd known Chase for years. A former Frank's Diner regular, he'd been one of the first Los Molinos residents who'd believed *her* side of the story, not Tommy's. She'd always be grateful for that. "But I don't think he's happy about it."

"No?"

She shook her head. "I'm Jessie Monroe. The girl who supposedly ruined his cousin's life. I don't think he can see past that."

"Then he's a fool," Chase said. "All anyone has to do is spend five minutes with you to tell you're not bad."

"Tell that to Rand," she said, pursing her lips. "But his mom doesn't seem to have a problem with me. Not anymore, at least."

Chase smiled. "Martha, a wise old bird. She and the other biddies might drive me crazy, but they're good people."

Rand's mom, along with Flora Montgomery and Edith Reynolds, were considered the Los Molinos Biddy Brigade. "You could have knocked me over with a feather when Martha told me to go after her son."

Chase chuckled. "Martha's been wanting to marry Rand off for years. She's probably relieved he's finally showing interest in someone."

"I don't know how interested he is."

"Oh, I think he's interested," Chase said.

Jessie wasn't so certain.

When she finally tracked down Rand a few minutes later, he was with a blonde. A beautiful blonde with slim legs and dark blue eyes that matched the headband she wore to keep her hair off her face. She wore a thick jacket—also dark blue—and even though the fluffy down covered her figure, Jessie could tell she had a body to match her tiny little legs.

Oh, great.

Rand looked up right then, eyes narrowing. The blonde followed his gaze.

"I was wondering what I'm supposed to be doing," Jessie said, trying not to gawk at the woman. She was one of those people so pretty you kind of had to stare just to take it all in. Flawless skin. Well, okay, maybe there were a few freckles sprinkled across the bridge of her nose. But she had the high cheekbones usually found on Barbies and china dolls.

"Just hang out for now," Rand said, turning to the woman. "Jayne, have you met Jessie?"

"No," she said in a sweet voice, a wide smile spreading across her face.

Ooh, look. She has a tooth a bit crooked— maybe she isn't perfect.

And maybe Jessie should stop being so catty.

"She's my new assistant," Rand announced, when Jessie didn't move.

"Oh," the woman said, her eyes lighting up. "Rand was just telling me about you."

"Really?" Jessie brushed a strand of hair off her face.

"Jayne asked how Peanut was."

"Rand tells me he couldn't have done that surgery without you."

Jessie shrugged. She wanted to hate the woman…wished Jayne would give her the once-over, maybe throw her a catty look, too. But she didn't, probably because she didn't feel threatened by Jessie. Some women were just so darn pretty they could afford to be sweet to everybody.

"He's just being nice," Jessie said, holding out her hand and forcing a smile to her stiff lips. "It's great to meet you, Jayne."

"You, too," she replied. "I'm so glad Rand's

finally found someone to help at the clinic." She turned back to him. "Now maybe you and I can go to dinner again."

Don't say it… Do *not* say it.

"That'd be nice," he said.

Why'd he have to go and say that?

Jessie didn't want to be reminded that there were other women Rand might be interested in. Women who were three times as gorgeous as her, and kind to boot.

"Are you going to the dance?" Jayne asked.

"Sure," Rand said.

"We are?"

The words were out of Jessie's mouth before she could stop them. Only too late did she realize that they'd come out sounding wrong. Sort of…possessive.

"I mean—" she felt her face heat up like a hot plate "—you are?"

"I was planning on it," Rand said.

But he hadn't told her about it. Jessie could think of only one reason why he wouldn't. He didn't want her there.

"When is it?"

"Tonight," Jayne said. "It's for the rodeo contestants, but all the rodeo personnel come, too. It's held over there." She pointed toward the grandstand and a massive white tent that had been erected nearby. "There's a live band and barbecue tri-tip and a bar. You should come. It'll be fun."

There was nothing Jessie despised more than a beautiful woman who was gracious, too. All right, that wasn't really true. She wanted to despise Jayne, she really did. Only she couldn't. To make matters worse, she realized Jayne and Rand made a cute couple.

The tightening in her stomach had nothing to do with the mention of tri-tip steaks.

"Are you sure it's okay if I come?" she asked Jayne, because she knew what Rand's answer would be.

"Of course."

"Great," Jessie said. "I think I just might take you up on that offer."

Chapter Eleven

Rand knew the night would bring trouble.

The moment Jessie had stood near Jayne, he'd recognized the stark differences between the two. Jayne might be beautiful to look at, but Jessie had a fire in her eyes that drew his gaze time and time again. There were no sweet or coy looks from her. She met him head-on, challenging him in a way that made Rand want to challenge her right back.

And then she arrived at the dance looking hotter than a barroom dancer.

He had no idea where she got the clothes, except he had a feeling Lani Cavenaugh had something to do with it. Chase's wife walked in with Jessie, a look of pride on her face as she observed the crowd's reaction, or more appropriately, the men's reactions.

Well, if she was trying to get Jessie noticed, she'd succeeded.

"Hot damn," one of the men murmured, staring at Jessie's bare, tan legs, plainly visible thanks to a short denim skirt. They had the sculpted elegance of a racehorse's long limbs.

Hot damn was right. Once again her breasts pushed against a long-sleeved shirt, this one maroon, a concho belt hugging her waist. She wore brown cowboy boots with rhinestones sewn into the toe and calf.

Lani's again. Rand would bet his truck on it.

"You look like you've been snakebit," Chase said after breaking away from his wife. Rand suspected he was trying conceal a smile, at least if the twitching of his mouth was any indication.

"You can tell your wife mission accomplished. Jessie'll be the talk of the rodeo."

"Well, I sure do hope so. Those two spent hours getting ready."

And as luck would have it, Jayne entered the tent then, her long denim skirt and blue-and-white checked shirt dowdy by comparison.

"Man, oh, man," he heard Chase drawl. "Have you got it bad."

"Huh?" Rand said.

His friend just shook his head, crossing his arms over the front of his white button-down. He wore a black cowboy hat similar to Rand's, only his was more battered.

"I'd have laid odds that you'd settle down with someone like Jayne over there," Chase said. "But after seeing the way you look at Jessie, I guess I'm wrong."

"You're not wrong. Jessie's my assistant, Chase. Nothing more."

"Keep telling yourself that, buddy." Chase's smile broke free. "Just keep on telling yourself that. Oh, look. Jake Barnes is sidling up to Jessie. He ought to show her a good time."

"What?" Sure enough, the rough stock rider walked right up to Lani and Jessie. "Hey, Jake," Rand heard Lani say. "Have you met Jessie?"

"No, but I'm hoping you'll remedy that situation," Jake declared.

Rand started moving toward them before he could stop himself. "Excuse me," he said to Chase.

"Yup," his friend stated. "Got it bad."

Rand ignored him.

"Rand," Lani said when she caught sight of him.

"Lani," Rand answered, ignoring Jake. "Jessie, can I talk to you?"

He thought he saw her lips twitch, "Sure. But Jake here just asked me to dance."

"He can wait," Rand said.

"Hey," Jake exclaimed. "Maybe I don't want to wait."

"You'll live," Rand said, grabbing Jessie by the hand.

"Rand," she protested.

But she followed him out the door, if one wanted to call the tent flaps that were pulled back a door. Outside the air felt heavier, as if it was about to rain.

"I'm surprised you didn't just drag me off by the hair."

"I need to talk to you," he said, pulling her around the corner of the tent.

"About what?"

"That horse that got injured today."

"You dragged me all the way outside to ask me about a horse's leg wrap?"

No, he'd dragged her outside because he didn't like the idea of her dancing with Jake. "Did you get it done?"

"I did," she said.

"Good."

She stood there, her face illuminated by a

nearby light. "Why don't you just admit the truth," she said softly.

"What truth?"

"That you get jealous as hell whenever another man comes near me." She lifted her chin.

"No, I don't."

"Yes, you do," she said. "And I'll be honest in admitting I felt the same way when you were talking to Jayne whatever her name is."

She had?

"Only unlike you, I'm not going to fight it anymore." She cleared her throat, moistened her lips with the tip of her tongue. "The question is, are you?"

And there she went, confronting things head-on. He wanted to walk back into the tent, but didn't have the willpower. He didn't want to fight this any more than she did.

"Jessie, it wouldn't be right to get involved with you."

"Why not?" she asked. "We're both adults. We're both attracted to each other."

The band started to play. Rand had to raise his voice to be heard. "Because I don't operate that way."

"Well, I do."

Suddenly she closed the distance between them. "Kiss me, Rand."

He told himself not to. Told himself to move away. He didn't.

When she reached up and gently pulled his head down, he didn't resist that, either. And when she pressed her body against his, he didn't pull back.

Their lips connected and everything went haywire.

His mind seemed to blank out so that all that was left were tactile sensations: the way her lips felt against his own—soft near the edges and then harder toward the middle, as if they might be chapped. The way her nose lightly touched the tip of his. The way she tasted.

She opened her mouth, just a little, as if inviting him to take it the rest of the way. He slipped his tongue between her lips and pulled her to him. More sensations flooded his awareness. How full her breasts felt against his chest. How warm her body was. How good she felt against him, there…right there.

He kissed her again, groaning at the way she responded to him.

"Mmm," she moaned.

That barely audible sound had him hotter than a dog in heat. He slid his hands down her arms, then let them drop even lower, to her hips, then

between their bodies. But when he moved his hand
to the apex of her thighs, she tensed.

He pulled back. "What's wrong?"

He saw surprise in her green eyes.

He ran his hands back up her arms. She tensed
again. "Jessie," he said. "I'd have to be dumb not
to sense the way you just froze."

"I didn't freeze," she said, stretching up on tiptoe and angling her head for another kiss.

He wasn't proof against a direct assault. And
when she reached out and touched him, running
her hand up his chest, he figured he must have
imagined it. Then she opened her mouth again, and
he forgot all about what he thought he'd felt,
unable to focus on anything other than the unbear-
able need to get close to her.

He felt her fingers move toward the center of his
chest. One of his buttons sprang free. She undid
another one, her hand skating over his pecs, the
hairs there charged by static wherever her fingers
glided. She moved her hand from side to side,
stroking him, and Rand mimicked the motion with
his tongue, losing himself in the rhythm of it all.
She knew how to touch him in just the right way.

He wrapped his arms around her and pulled her
against his arousal.

She definitely tensed.

He might have missed it if she hadn't been touching him, might have missed the way her hand momentarily paused. But he didn't.

"Something's not right," he said, staring down at her. "And I wish to God I knew what it was."

Chapter Twelve

How could he know?

How could he have possibly figured it out?

She forced a smile. "Nothing's wrong, Rand. Everything feels perfectly right."

"Bull."

"No, it's true—"

To her shock, he stepped back. "Every time I touch you, you freeze up."

No, she didn't. She hadn't done that in years. "You're imagining things," she said, taking a step toward him.

But he didn't bend down. Didn't close the distance between them. Instead he stepped away from her, crossing to the corner of the tent and then turning to face her.

"What happened?"

She felt her spine grow rigid. "What do you mean?"

He lifted his cowboy hat and ran his hand through his hair. "Jessie, I've been healing animals for years. Long enough to have an instinct about people, too. Something happened in the past that gave you scars. I can sense it. You might try to hide it, but I can see right through you."

Her heart had started to pound like a panicked bird that wanted to escape. She did want to escape, she realized. Suddenly, she wanted to turn and run.

"I don't know what you're talking about." Even to her own ears, her voice sounded wooden and detached.

"Who hurt you?"

She thought about denying it, thought about telling him nobody had hurt her, but like an animal backed into a corner, she lashed out. "You know who hurt me."

He didn't flinch, didn't react at all. "No," he said. "I don't know."

"Think, Rand. Think back to when Tommy was arrested. Think about my side of the story."

He leaned away, his shoulders stiff. "Tommy?"

"Tommy." She crossed her arms in front of her.

"But the police never charged him with rape."

"Because there wasn't enough evidence. Rough sex, they called it, and given my reputation…"

There'd been enough reasonable doubt for them to offer Tommy a deal: confess to possession charges and they'd drop the attempted rape, which, as the D.A. had explained to Jessie, was better all around. Tommy would go to jail and she wouldn't have to face him in court.

"Tommy would never hurt a woman like that."

"Just like he would never sell drugs, I suppose. Or manufacture them. It was *me* who could do those bad things. Me who ruined *Tommy's* life. Me who was the bad influence all those years ago."

And still, *still* Rand looked incredulous.

"Grow up!" she said, furious with herself for being so forward and throwing herself at him. After all they'd been through together, he still didn't believe her.

"Jessie," he called when she walked toward the entrance of the tent.

"For someone who proclaims to be intuitive, you can be awfully dense," she said before heading back inside.

She left him standing there, a look of stunned disbelief on his face.

SHE WAS STILL ANGRY at him the next morning. The rodeo wasn't due to start until that afternoon, so she'd called Rand's room and left him a message saying she'd find her own way out to the grounds. Chase and Lani were only too happy to pick her up.

But she wouldn't be able to avoid Rand at the rodeo.

It had turned warmer by midafternoon, and Jessie was glad for the shade of the tall trees. Her feet scuffed across pine needles and oak leaves as she made her way from the parking lot to the rodeo grounds with the Cavanaughs, their kids running ahead as if just released from prison.

"They love rodeos," Lani said.

"I can see that."

Chase had his arm around Lani, a smile on his face as he watched Rose grab her brother by the hand.

"It's Rose who wants to ride," Lani said. "I told Chase she's going to be riding bulls before too long."

"Not if I can help it," Chase said, pausing as his cell phone rang.

"Hey, Rand," he said a second later.

Jessie fumbled with her purse strap.

"Yup. She's right here." Chase looked amused beneath his tan cowboy hat. "I'll tell her."

"Tell me what?" Jessie said when he'd disconnected.

"Rand needs your help. Guess he's vaccinating some of Taylor's bulls this morning, the ones he decided not to use for competition."

"Vaccinating?" Jessie asked. "Now?"

"It's actually pretty common to inoculate rodeo stock on the road. The animals are so rarely home, and if they are, it's too much of a pain to herd them up and run them through. Easier to do routine vet work when you've got them penned."

"Then I guess I better go."

"Jessie," Lani said as she turned away. "Don't let him scare you off."

Jessie didn't pretend not to know what her friend was talking about. "Oh, I won't," she said with a smile.

But she lied. She was more nervous than a frog in a pool of piranhas as she made her way toward the bull pens. The Hamilton Hills Rodeo Grounds lay at the base of a mountain, the trees beyond so thick that from a distance they looked like an uneven green rug. But the place was beautiful. Peaceful. Or at least it should have been peaceful. As Jessie rounded the rodeo arena, she felt anything but at peace.

"Hey," she said when she arrived, giving Rand a tentative smile.

Nothing.

He stared down at her with the cool detachment of a doctor examining a patient. She didn't know what disappointed her more—that he'd had a whole night to think about what she'd told him, and still didn't appear to believe her, or that he didn't even have the decency to smile in greeting.

"They need their vaccinations," Rand said. "I'll need your help working the chutes."

"Sure." She swallowed hard.

He spoke so gently to his four-legged patients that it was all she could do not to pull him aside and ask him to treat her like that.

"Here, let me help you," said a lanky cowboy with a grin as big as the invitation in his eyes. He tried to take the plastic bat she was using to push the bull forward.

"No, thanks. I've got it," she said.

"You sure?" he asked. "These boys can be tough to handle." And judging by his tone of voice, it wasn't the bull he was talking about.

"You might be surprised what I can handle." She hadn't meant that to come out sounding so flirtatious. Or maybe she had. At this point it was hard to tell what was real and what was an act. One thing was certain: Rand wasn't happy.

"Do you guys mind helping me out here?" he called from the other side of the chute.

"You're going to get me in trouble," she mumbled to the cowboy.

"So?" His brown eyes twinkled, tiny tufts of blond hair poking out from beneath the brim of his battered straw hat.

"So," Jessie said, starting to grow uncomfortable, "it's my job to help Dr. Sheppard, and I don't want to get fired."

"Weren't you at the dance last night?" he asked, ignoring her protest.

"I was," she said with a polite smile. "Now, if you'll excuse me."

She turned her back to the man, shaking the plastic baseball bat at the bull. There were rocks inside the thing and, as ludicrous as it might seem, the sound of them scared the three-thousand-pound bull into moving forward.

"Sorry about that," Jessie said to Rand.

"Careful," he called to her as the brown-and-white Hereford cross suddenly went ballistic. Jessie backed up a step at the bull's enraged bellow. The big animal was trying to escape by any means possible. The fencing was as high as her head, but that didn't stop the bull from trying. Once he realized he couldn't leap over, back up or pry his way out beneath the six-inch boards, he settled down.

Jessie shook the bat again, her hands trembling. But the bull walked forward. That didn't reassure her much. This particular bull had horns, the sharp ends filed off so as not to harm his handlers—or a rider who happened to fall off in his path. Jessie gave those horns a wide birth as she pushed the bull into the short chute.

"Pass me that rope," Rand said.

She gulped, not at all happy about having to put her hand in the chute.

"Just toss it toward me," he said.

But he sounded so impatient, Jessie passed the rope over the bull's back.

Rand gave her a look. "Wrap the rope around that board there," he said, passing the hemp line back in her direction. "Then toss it over to me. And I mean toss, Jessie. Don't put your hands in the chute."

"Got it," she said a few seconds later, doing as asked.

She sighed in relief when they had the bull tied

down. "We've only got a few to do," he said, pushing the end of a plunger down, ridding the syringe of air in preparation for injection. Fluid shot out the end of the wicked-looking needle.

"Okay," he said after injecting the bull and untying his end of the rope. "Let him go."

Jessie loosened her end and the big bull went on his way.

"Next," Rand said.

Her cowboy admirer had left, Jessie saw, as she and Rand pushed the next bull through the chutes. They followed the same routine as before. Jessie felt she'd gotten the hang of it by the third animal.

That must have been why she wasn't paying close attention as she helped undo the rope from over the fourth bull's back.

The stupid animal ducked backward just as she unwrapped the rope, catching her on the hand before she could pull away.

"Damn it!" She glanced down at the wide gouge.

"What?" Rand asked. "What happened?"

"Nothing," she lied. "Just a small scratch." A cut that had already started to bleed. Profusely. Damn it. This was all she needed. Rand was undoubtedly waiting for an excuse to fire her, especially after last night, and now she'd gone and done something incredibly stupid.

He was up and over the top of the chute before she could turn away. "Let me see," he said, his expression harsh as he grabbed her arm and turned it toward him.

"Ouch!"

"Sorry," he muttered. "Shoot, Jessie. That's hardly a scratch."

"It'll be okay with some soap and water."

She could tell he wasn't happy. But she saw something else in his eyes, something that took her by surprise and—all right, she could admit it— made her catch her breath. He was concerned.

"C'mon," he said.

Of course he looked concerned, Jessie thought. He was a doctor. Well, an animal doctor. And she was his employee.

"What about Hummer there?" she said, nodding toward the bull.

"Hummer can wait." He grabbed her by the other arm and led her away.

"What happened?" someone asked as they headed toward Rand's truck, blood trickling off the end of her thumb.

"Got scraped by a horn," Rand said.

The grizzled old cowboy pushed his hat back. "You need me to get Doc over here?"

Rand glanced at her wound again. "Nah. I think we'll do just fine with peroxide and water."

"Peroxide," Jessie said. "Oh, no. You're not putting peroxide on that."

"Yes, we are," he said, stopping at the back of his truck.

"No, really. It's just a scratch—"

"It's more than a scratch. Exactly how much more we'll find out after I clean it up."

"Seriously, it'll be okay."

He looked amused. "Why, Jessie Monroe, you're not afraid of a little peroxide, are you?"

She swallowed. "Yes," she admitted in a small voice. And the thing was, she was absolutely serious. She hated the stuff. It gave her the heebie-jeebies every time she smelled it.

"Close your eyes," he said.

"Oh, jeez." She did as he asked.

Jessie heard him open a drawer. Heard him rummage around.

Thu-thump, thu-thump went her heart.

She heard him unscrew a lid.

"Ready?" he asked. "One…two…"

She braced herself.

But the bastard didn't wait for three.

"Holy!" She jumped back, nearly crashing into the truck, her hand stinging so badly tears came to her eyes. "Ouch, ouch, ouch," she cried, jumping up and down and shaking her hand. "Wow…that *stings*."

"Yeah, but not that much," he said.

"Easy for you to say."

"Let me have a look."

"No," she retorted. "Not after that stunt."

"Jessie," he said, taking her arm and giving her a reassuring smile. "The worst is over."

"That's what Dr. Frankenstein said just before he shot a million volts through his poor creation's body."

"Let me have a look."

She reluctantly held out her hand.

His touch was gentle and somehow calming. It reminded her of the other night, of how it felt to be in his arms. Of how good it'd felt to kiss him.

"Hmm," he said, drawing her attention.

"Will I need stitches?"

"Nope. But it'll need some cleaning up."

"Great," Jessie muttered.

"It won't hurt as bad now. The peroxide's done its worst."

"It's not the peroxide I'm worried about now, it's the cleaning."

His grip tightened, but just for a second, the gesture meant to reassure her. "I promise to be gentle."

She looked up into his eyes. "I know," she said.

"Let me get some gauze."

She swallowed. Her heart had started to buck in her chest again. "Rand!"

He turned, and there was something in his eyes, something that made her think he might sense what was coming next.

"About last night—"

"No," he said with a shake of his head. "I was the one that was an ass."

"Yes, you were."

He burst out laughing. "And I know you well enough by now to know you wouldn't say anything without good reason," he was finally able to get out. "Look, I'm not saying I don't believe you right now. Part of me does. But part of me…"

"Doesn't," Jessie finished for him.

"But I promise you this. I'm going to have a talk with Tommy."

"Really?" she said.

Rand stared at her for a long moment. "Really."

Chapter Thirteen

They returned home the next evening, she and Rand having arrived at a sort of unspoken truce. He didn't make any overt gestures toward renewing their physical intimacy, but he wasn't withdrawn, either.

When they arrived back at the vet clinic he said a polite goodbye. Jessie paused for a moment with her hand on the door. He didn't move toward her, didn't lean forward in a way that made her think he might try to kiss her goodbye.

She'd never felt more confused in her life about a man than she did at that moment. Confused and bewildered and, all right, a little scared. If she was this out of her depth, what would it be like if they'd been intimate?

She had the next day off because of working

through the weekend, and even though she told herself she wasn't going to wait by the phone, that's exactly what ended up happening. Only Rand didn't call.

So when she reported to work the next morning—the injury on the back of her hand looking like nothing more than a scratch—she wasn't sure what to expect. It certainly wasn't the pleasant man who greeted her and asked if she'd had a nice day off, and then acted as if nothing had ever happened between them. Rand's behavior left her even more confused.

It was one of those days where the stars and the moons not only didn't align, they were a million, trillion galaxies away from each other. She was so engrossed in injecting a painkiller into the horse that had come in lame that she didn't hear someone approach. And when she looked up, it was too late.

Tommy.

She almost dropped the syringe. During all their years living in the same town, they'd managed to avoid each other.

Until now.

"What do you want?" she asked, turning her back on him and giving the horse a pat, her heart thumping in her chest.

The Harlequin Reader Service® — Here's how it works:

Accepting your 2 free books and 2 free mystery gifts places you under no obligation to buy anything. You may keep the books and gifts and return the shipping statement marked "cancel." If you do not cancel, about a month later we'll send you 4 additional books and bill you just $4.24 each in the U.S., or $4.99 each in Canada, plus 25¢ shipping & handling per book and applicable taxes if any.* That's the complete price and — compared to cover prices of $4.99 each in the U.S. and $5.99 each in Canada — it's quite a bargain! You may cancel at any time, but if you choose to continue, every month we'll send you 4 more books, which you may either purchase at the discount price or return to us and cancel your subscription.

*Terms and prices subject to change without notice. Sales tax applicable in N.Y. Canadian residents will be charged applicable provincial taxes and GST. All orders subject to approval. Credit or debit balances in a customer's account(s) may be offset by any other outstanding balance owed by or to the customer. Please allow 4 to 6 weeks for delivery.

If offer card is missing write to: Harlequin Reader Service, 3010 Walden Ave., P.O. Box 1867, Buffalo NY 14240-1867

NO POSTAGE
NECESSARY
IF MAILED
IN THE
UNITED STATES

BUSINESS REPLY MAIL
FIRST-CLASS MAIL   PERMIT NO. 717-003   BUFFALO, NY

POSTAGE WILL BE PAID BY ADDRESSEE

HARLEQUIN READER SERVICE
3010 WALDEN AVE
PO BOX 1867
BUFFALO NY 14240-9952

GET FREE BOOKS and FREE GIFTS
WHEN YOU PLAY THE...

Lucky 7

SLOT MACHINE GAME!

Just scratch off the silver box with a coin. Then check below to see the gifts you get!

YES! I have scratched off the silver box. Please send me the 2 free Harlequin American Romance® books and 2 free gifts for which I qualify. I understand I am under no obligation to purchase any books, as explained on the back of this card.

354 HDL EF4V   **154 HDL EF4P**

FIRST NAME	LAST NAME

ADDRESS

APT.#	CITY

STATE/PROV.	ZIP/POSTAL CODE

7	7	7	**Worth TWO FREE BOOKS plus 2 BONUS Mystery Gifts!**
🍒	🍒	🍒	**Worth TWO FREE BOOKS!**
♣	♣	♣	**Worth ONE FREE BOOK!**
🔔	🔔	🍒	**TRY AGAIN!**

www.eHarlequin.com

(H-AR-12/06)

Offer limited to one per household and not valid to current Harlequin American Romance® subscribers.

Your Privacy - Harlequin Books is committed to protecting your privacy. Our Privacy Policy is available online at www.eHarlequin.com or upon request from the Harlequin Reader Service. From time to time we make our lists of customers available to reputable firms who may have a product or service of interest to you. If you would prefer for us not to share your name and address, please check here ☐.

"Now see here, Jessie. Is that any way to greet your long-lost boyfriend?"

She felt ill. Yet she had nothing to fear from him. He'd tried his best to ruin her once before and had failed. He wouldn't succeed now.

"I would prefer it if you stayed long-lost," she said, wiping away a spot of blood on the horse's neck before turning back to him. She busied herself putting the cap back on the needle.

"You're just saying that 'cause you're still sore at me."

She smirked, pushing the stall door open. "Gee, you think I have a reason to be sore?"

She tried to walk past him, but his hand snaked out to stop her. She stepped back, not even having to think twice as she lifted her leg and kneed him in the groin.

"Ooooph," he groaned, doubling over in pain.

She'd been waiting years to do that.

"I'm not a naive seventeen-year-old anymore, Tommy, and nobody, but *nobody,* touches me without my invitation anymore."

Slowly, she walked by. Let him stand there in the middle of the barn aisle and rot.

"I can make trouble for you," he called.

"Go ahead."

She could hear his feet shuffle on the rubber mats that kept horses from sliding on the barn's concrete floor. Jessie ignored him. But as she headed toward the surgical room, she paused. Rand was still inside. At least he should be.

She put her hand on the sliding door, opened it just a crack and then turned back to Tommy. "You've already made enough trouble for me to last a lifetime."

Anger burned in his eyes. "Not near as much trouble as I can cause you now," he said. "At least if the rumors about you and my cousin are to be believed."

"And what rumors are those?" she asked, hoping against hope Rand was inside the room, and that he recognized Tommy's voice. And that he'd stay in there long enough to hear—

"That you and he are together."

"And what business is it of yours if we are?"

"You know why dating Rand is a bad idea."

She lifted her chin. "Ah, yes. I remember now. You're afraid your despicable behavior will come to light."

He didn't say anything, and she knew that's exactly what he thought. "You know as well as I do Rand will believe me over you," he finally muttered.

"Because you're such a perfect angel. The preacher's son who was led down the garden path by Los Molinos's version of Eve."

"That's right."

Jessie wanted to knee him in the groin again. "You know, I really would have thought five years in jail would have done you some good."

"Five years I spent in jail no thanks to you."

"Hey, *I* didn't put those drugs in your glove compartment."

"That's not what your boyfriend thinks."

She tipped her head to the side as she studied him. "And I'm long past caring what people think of me. I'm happy with myself. If you think coming here to threaten me will keep me quiet, you're sadly mistaken."

He gave her a hard stare back. "Then I guess you'll learn yet again that when it comes to credibility, you have none."

"And I guess you're going to learn that the truth always comes out," another masculine voice said.

Jessie turned.

Rand.

JESSIE STEPPED BACK as Rand slid open the surgical room door.

"Rand," Tommy said, his blue eyes filled with guilt. And then he blinked the guilt away. He did it so fast, it was impressive, and all the more troubling.

"I'm sure your father would be interested in the truth, too."

"Not after I tell him you and Jessie are sleeping together."

Rand took a step toward him. "For the record, we are *not* sleeping together." Not yet, at least. "And I'll make sure your father knows that, too."

"He won't believe you," his cousin said.

"Oh, I think he will," Rand countered. "Especially since Pauline heard the whole conversation, too."

Rand motioned to the open door and Pauline stepped cautiously out. She looked from Jessie to his cousin. He couldn't be sure, but he thought he saw remorse in her expression.

No more than he felt.

"Go home, Tommy, but tell your father I'll be paying him a call." Actually, he'd already paid him a call, but maybe Uncle Phil would listen to what he had to say this time.

"He won't believe you," Tommy repeated, though he didn't sound quite so confident. So...cocky.

"We'll just have to see about that, won't we?"

Tommy looked as if he might say something else, then his face hardened and he turned away.

"Thanks," Jessie said softly.

"No need to thank me." Rand glanced over at Pauline, who quickly turned and left.

"No. I appreciate you sticking up for me like that."

Rand let out a huff. "Jessie, I pride myself on being a fair and honest man. To say I'm horrified by what I just overheard would be an understatement."

She didn't flinch. "It's not easy when people betray your trust."

"No, it's not." He shook his head, the ramifications of what he'd just heard settling over him. "But you learned that lesson long ago."

"I did," she said, straightening her shoulders. It was a stance that seemed all too familiar. How many times had he watched her square off against the people of Los Molinos? Not that the whole town knew who she was, or even cared about her past. But some people still remembered. Some people still treated her like a pariah.

Including him.

"Ah, jeez, Jessie," he said, running a hand through his hair. "I've been such an ass."

"Uh-huh."

And there was that cocky smile, her flippant

remark yet another self-defense mechanism he recognized. "That's my Jessie," he said. "Honest to a fault."

"That I am," she said, pushing away from the wall and swiftly moving past him.

"Jessie, wait." She flinched when he grabbed her hand, and Rand remembered too late about her injury. "You okay?" he asked.

"Fine."

He looked down at the red line on her hand, his stomach churning. And it wasn't because it looked bad. Actually, it looked fine.

"I'm sorry," he said. And he wasn't just talking about her injury.

"No need to apologize," she said softly.

She wore the same T-shirt as she had her first day of work, a threadbare cotton garment

"Yes, Jessie, I do need to apologize. I've behaved badly. Not just recently, but for years."

"It's okay," she said with another smile. But behind the cocky devil-may-care expression lurked a terrible vulnerability. "What you said was no worse than what a lot of people in this town still say about me."

"I thought myself a better judge of character than that."

"I trusted Tommy once upon a time, too."

"Do you mind telling me what really happened?"

She broke eye contact. "Actually, I do." She shrugged. "Maybe later, when I've calmed down. Seeing Tommy always gets me riled."

Rand let her go, hadn't even realized he'd still been holding her. "I guess I can understand that."

"Besides," she said, "we've got work to do, Dr. Sheppard."

And she was too professional to let it slide. Amazing how he hadn't seen that before.

"Will you let me take you to dinner tonight?"

"Maybe," she said, walking into the surgical room. "We'll have to see how the day goes."

Which was as close to a brush-off as he'd ever heard.

"You coming?" she asked, stopping in the middle of the room.

"Not just yet," he said. "I have to pay a call on my uncle. Think you can handle the vaccinations we have scheduled for this afternoon?"

"I do."

"Good," he said, giving her a smile.

She didn't seem to notice.

"Have Pauline page me if there's an emergency."

"Will do," Jessie said with a lift of her hand.

She disappeared into the office. He stood there, staring at the spot where she'd been.

"Son of a bitch," he muttered. His left boot heel ground into the rubber mat beneath his foot. "Son of a bitch."

It became all too clear in that instant that he'd blown it with Jessie Monroe.

The question was, how did he repair the damage?

Chapter Fourteen

It was amazing how quickly Pauline's attitude changed. It was as if someone had waved a magic wand. Abracadabra and the wicked stepsister was gone.

"We've got two vaccinations coming in this afternoon," she said, handing Jessie some charts. "After that the schedule's clear."

It was the first time Pauline had ever handed a case over to her. Granted, Rand was about to leave the clinic, but Jessie hadn't told her that.

"Thanks," she said.

"Jessie—" the woman started to say.

"Don't, Pauline." Jessie lifted a hand. "One apology per day is more than enough."

The receptionist nodded, seeming to understand Jessie's reluctance to hear her out.

They both looked up as a customer came in, a cat mewling in protest. "Which room for the vaccinations?"

"Room three."

Jessie turned, lifting the charts in acknowledgment.

RAND DIDN'T RETURN TO THE CLINIC. Pauline informed her that he was out on business for the rest of the day. Jessie was almost relieved to hear the news.

Still, as she drove home later that evening, she expected to see his truck parked out in front of her apartment—and wouldn't that scandalize some of the old-timers who still hung out their doors to see who came by to visit her? To be honest, Jessie was worried Tommy might be lying in wait for her. But the cars out in front of the drab complex were the same ones as always.

Despite reassuring herself that she didn't want to hear from Rand, she still listened for the phone when she took a shower that night, still traipsed over to the answering machine to see if the incoming-message light was blinking. One message, from her mom. Jessie decided to call her back later, although she did wonder what she was phoning about. Probably needed money. Some things never changed. And when the phone rang a half hour later, Jessie's pulse raced. Only it wasn't Rand, it was *his* mother.

"Hello, Jessie," Martha said brightly. "It's Martha Sheppard here."

"Is Rand all right?" Jessie asked. She'd been worried about him. Not that she expected Tommy to do something stupid, but you never knew...

"Rand? Why, of course Rand's all right. At least I think he is. I talked to him just a short while ago and he seemed fine."

That was a relief. But if Rand was okay, what was Martha doing calling her?

"Say, listen," the woman said. "As you know, we run a guest ranch here at the Diamond W. Every evening we have a country-style dinner and I was wondering if maybe you wanted to join us tonight. I'm big on having even numbers, and with Rand missing today, that left me short a spot. Do you mind filling in?"

Jessie was rendered speechless for all of five seconds. "Excuse me?" she finally said.

"I like to have an even number of people at the table—"

"No, no," Jessie said, shaking her head. A fat

strand of hair slopped into her eyes. She brushed it away. "I heard you."

I'm just having a hard time believing it.

"But, um, I'm not so sure I can make it."

"Big date tonight?" Martha asked.

For a second Jessie thought about lying, but Mrs. Sheppard seemed to have eyes and ears all over Los Molinos. Likely as not she knew someone who knew someone who lived in Jessie's apartment complex. That someone would let Martha know that Jessie was a bald-faced liar. Up until a few weeks ago, that's exactly what Martha had thought, anyway. "No, I, um. It's just that some of my favorite television shows are on tonight."

"No problem. We've got TiVo. I'll be sure to record them."

They had *what* at the ranch?

"Dinner's at seven."

"Seven—"

"We eat a bit later in the summer. Come early if you like."

And that was that. Or at least that was the end of the conversation. Martha had hung up on her.

"Did she fall for it?" Flora asked.

Martha stared into the faces of her oldest

friends, Flora and Edith. Well, not old as in *old* old. Martha had a good three years on Flora. But they'd all stopped counting after their sixtieths.

"She's coming," Martha said, flopping down on one of two claw-footed sofas, the dark green furniture arranged facing each other.

"Doesn't sound like you gave her much of a choice," Edith said from her own perch on a matching armchair.

Edith was the pacifist of the three. She always worried about other people's feelings, goodness knew why.

"The question is, will *Rand* fall in with your plan," Flora said as she turned away from the gauze-covered window, her brightly dyed red brows drawn upward.

She should know better by now.

"He will," Martha said. "Especially after our conversation this afternoon."

"I still can't believe little Tommy did that to poor Jessie," Edith said, looking top-heavy with a long braid coiled around her head.

"*Little* Tommy is lucky I don't beat his ass."

"*Flora*," Martha said. "Watch your mouth. I have guests wandering around here."

They all looked toward the entry hall. Martha's

home was huge, and this time of day most of the guests were up in their rooms resting after a busy day. But Martha still got up to check, slowly. Her bones were so worn she popped and crackled like a campfire.

No one in the hallway. Just as she suspected.

"Okay, we have an hour to figure out what we're going to do."

"God help us," Flora said.

"Actually, I think it'd be better if God helped Rand," Edith said softly. "Rand's the one who has Martha for a mother."

JESSIE STILL COULDN'T believe she'd been invited to dinner at the Diamond W. For years she'd wondered what the inside of the place looked like. Now, it appeared as if she'd find out.

She parked in front of the antebellum-style mansion. The horseshoe-shaped driveway was empty, the guests out behind the house, apparently. It was hard to tell because the place was so huge. Three stories, surrounded by lots of large trees.

"There you are," Martha said, opening wide one of the double doors. Jessie hadn't even gotten to raise the antique lion's head knocker.

"Good evening, Mrs. Sheppard."

"Martha," she reminded her, stepping back to let her in.

Jessie tried not to hunch over as she entered. She always felt so inadequate around this woman. Martha always managed to look so cool and elegant. Like she did tonight, dressed in tan slacks and a silky top. Jessie felt woefully underdressed even though she'd worn her best pair of jeans and the second new article of clothing she'd bought in recent weeks: a black Lycra top under a gauzy black shirt that matched her black boots.

"Wow. It smells great in here," Jessie said, trying to make conversation. "Where should I put my purse?" She held up her battered brown bag.

Martha didn't move.

Jessie didn't either. "Or should I just hold on to it?" she asked.

"Actually, I have a confession to make."

Oh, jeez. From the look on her face, it wouldn't be good.

"I lied earlier. You're not really here to have dinner with my guests. You're here to have dinner with Rand."

Chapter Fifteen

Rand didn't expect her to show. If there was one thing he knew about Jessie it was that she liked to do things her way. Falling into step with his mother's plans didn't sound like her.

He shouldn't have underestimated his mother.

The lake was situated at the bottom of a small rise, a four-foot-wide path leading to it, used by guests in the cabins at the water's edge.

He heard her footsteps before he saw her. It was almost sunset, the sky drenched in sherbet-colored light. She stopped when she saw the boat and lights.

"Unreal," he thought he heard her murmur.

She hadn't spotted him yet, obviously. He sat on the steps of a vacant cabin, his arms resting on his knees.

"Do you like it?" he called.

She turned sharply. "I can't believe you put candles in a boat." Her hands on her hips, she turned back to the lake. "And lit them."

"I didn't," he said, walking toward her. He'd chosen not to wear a hat tonight, and he saw her gaze dart over his hair, probably because it was a mess. "Edith and Flora are up to their usual tricks."

"They're here, too?"

"Yup. You just missed them. I'm surprised you didn't see them walking up the path."

"They're probably in the bushes hiding."

Rand smiled. They probably were, along with his mother.

"It does look pretty, though."

"Yeah, but I wish they'd found a battery-operated lantern. This might go out when we set sail…not to mention the candles. If you're up for a picnic dinner, that is."

"Unbelievable," she repeated. "How big is this lake?"

"Almost two miles. Big enough to sail on, but not big enough to waterski, although my brother and I tried that once."

"I bet you did," she murmured.

"Are you hungry?"

"Famished."

"Good, because there's some of my mom's famous honey-pecan chicken, potato salad and a nice bottle of wine. Chardonnay. Kendal-Jackson."

"They thought of everything, didn't they?"

"Actually, I thought of the wine."

She looked back at the boat. "We really don't have to go out on the lake if you don't want to. I'm happy eating dinner on the steps of your cabin. It's pretty."

"You've never been here before, have you?"

She smiled. "Now when would I have had the opportunity?"

He felt like an idiot for reminding her of the past. "I'm sorry for not believing you."

She shrugged. "Hey, it's not like Tommy made it easy. He turned out to be a great actor."

"A regular Academy Award-winning performance," he said, squinting as he looked out over the water. "The guy pulled the wool over everyone's eyes."

"What happened when you went to see your uncle?"

"Tommy denied everything, but his father knows me too well not to believe me."

"It's hard for parents to think the worst of their children," she said, watching as the water lapped at the pebblestrewn shore near her feet. "And if Tommy keeps working on him…"

"Then I'll be disappointed in my uncle, but I suppose no more than I'm disappointed in my cousin."

She nodded.

"Will you tell me what happened back then? I asked Tommy, but he's still denying it all." Rand shook his head. "Even after I heard him say that stuff to you, he's still trying to deny it. Unbelievable."

"He's been doing that his whole life."

"So what happened?"

She shrugged. "Poor kid falls for rich kid. Rich kid pretends to be someone he's not to get what he wants. Poor kid gets her heart broken."

"It had to have been a little more than that."

"It was."

"If you'd rather keep it private, then keep it private."

"It's not that, it's just…" She brushed her hair back.

He waited. Her eyes scanned the horizon. The sun had started to turn the tops of the hills yellow, the lower portion an army-green.

"It's hard to talk about," she admitted.

The look in her eyes made him want to comfort her. "You don't have to talk about it, Jessie. Really."

"I know."

He touched her and her skin seemed cold. Or maybe that was his imagination. "Just tell me one thing," he said.

"What's that?"

"How bad did he hurt you?"

Chapter Sixteen

Goose bumps rose on Jessie's skin. "Bad enough," she said, lapsing into silence.

"Tell me," he prompted.

"The night he was arrested, he'd been drinking. A lot. He tried to get me to go to his room."

Rand looked...sad. "But you didn't want to go."

"I fought him off. He became enraged. I called him a jerk. He called me white trash. It was horrible."

"And so you walked out."

"I did. Well, ran, really." She hugged herself.

"And he chased after you."

A wave rolled in farther than any of the others, nearly touching her toes. "Not right away. I swear he let me get far enough away that he could do something to me without anyone seeing. There was malice in his eyes that night, Rand. He looked capable of doing worse than raping me." She wrapped her arms around herself, shivering.

Rand reached out and rubbed her shoulder. "I'm sorry."

"No. It was my own stupid fault. You reap what you sow, and I was sowing wild oats back then."

"But all these years I thought—"

"I know what you thought, and for good reason, too. I deserved my reputation. Tommy was good at concealing his dark side. *Really* good. When he claimed the drugs were mine, people believed him. It was his word against mine."

Rand shook his head. "You think you know someone…."

"It's like that with a lot of folks, Rand. My mom used to bring guys home who seemed so nice. But then they'd get too friendly with me. Or they'd start hitting my mom." Jessie released a breath. "I couldn't leave home fast enough."

"And now look at you."

"Now look at me," she said softly. "When I graduated, I was the oldest student in my class, but I did it."

"You did it," he echoed softly.

Tears came to her eyes. She didn't know why.

Well, maybe she did. He looked so proud. Of her, she realized.

"You're a very special woman."

"One of a kind," she said with a small smile.

He leaned toward her. Jessie didn't move. She couldn't. Her skin began to tingle. And when his breath wafted over her face, her lips began to tingle, too. She closed her eyes, anticipating, wanting….

There.

He kissed her, so softly at first she thought she might be imagining the contact. But then her lips turned warm beneath the heat of his own.

Yes.

This was what she wanted. Back-of-the-neck-tingling kisses that stirred her body and made her remember she was a woman, and Rand a man.

His hand dropped from her shoulder, skated down her arm. She felt the gentle brush of his thumb just below the swell of her breast. She wanted him to touch her. Wanted him to cup her and to maybe tip his head and kiss her—

"Don't," she said, pulling back.

"Jessie." He gasped for breath like a man who'd been underwater too long.

"Not here," she said. "Not now." She looked around them. It was almost dark. "I feel as if your mom and Flora and Edith are in the bushes out there, watching us."

"You're probably right," he said, clearly amused. "Come on. Let's go on our picnic."

IT WAS A MAGICAL boat ride, one Jessie would always remember. They glided across the smooth water, the lantern lighting the way, catching the edges of their wake and turning it silver. He followed the shoreline for a while, past cabins lit from within. There were quite a few of them, and Rand explained that they had guests year-round.

"How come you don't live in one of those cabins?" Jesse asked, trailing her hand in the water.

"Because it's too far from the clinic."

And that might make a difference in saving an animal's life. Of course. She should have guessed as much.

"Where are we going?" she asked.

"You'll see."

He sat at the bow, facing her, arms working the oars in a way that bespoke his expertise. Occasionally their gazes would meet and she could see him smile. She'd smile back, but the whole time her thoughts were racing.

Where was he taking her?

What would happen after they ate dinner?

Would they even get to eat?

Because there was no denying the tension in the air. It hung over the boat like an area of low pressure about to erupt into a storm.

"You cold?" he asked. "There's some blankets behind you."

"Nope. I'm not cold."

I'm hot. And nervous. And…scared.

Scared like she'd been that night outside the rodeo tent. Scared, she quickly realized, not because of memories of Tommy, but because of the way it felt whenever Rand kissed her—like they'd been kissing each other their whole lives.

"Here we are," he said.

She blinked, looked around. They were still off-shore.

"What—" And then she saw it. A diving platform, probably twenty feet long and thirty feet wide. Large enough to hold a bright blue slide and more than a few chaise lounges.

"Wow."

"We built it last year. Probably one of our better investments. The kids come here and have a blast. The parents get to lie in the sun."

The boat tipped to the right as they came up

against the rubber edge. Rand seemed to know exactly what he was doing, looping a rope around one of the cleats and then climbing out.

"Here," he said, offering her a hand. Good thing, too, because she wasn't nearly as agile as he was. When her feet hit the platform, she lost her balance.

And fell right into his arms.

"Careful there," he said softly.

She experienced the same rush of feeling she did whenever they touched. When he held her, she felt as if nothing would ever be the same again.

"Thanks," she said softly.

"Jessie," he murmured.

They wouldn't be eating dinner. At least not right away. She'd known that the moment she stepped into the boat.

She raised herself up on tiptoe, pulled his head down…and kissed him.

It was no tender kiss this time.

Their attraction burst loose from its confinement. Their tongues touched, and Jessie almost sank to the deck.

RAND HEARD HER MOAN, felt her body grow still for a second before she pressed up against him. Her breasts pushed into his chest, and Rand lifted a hand and cupped one. No bra. Or maybe one of those satin ones. He didn't know, didn't care, just relished the way it felt to hold her so intimately.

His mouth seemed to have a will of its own, leaving her lips to nibble at her ear, then dropping lower so he could nip the crook of her neck. She pressed into him, tipping her head sideways as she moaned his name. But he wasn't through kissing her. Lower and lower he went, sinking to his knees and pressing his mouth against her warm mound.

"Oh, jeez."

His hand lifted to her jeans.

"Rand, don't—"

"Shh," he said, popping the button loose. Her zipper slid open with a metallic ting, her white underwear exposed beneath.

"No, really—"

"Shh," he repeated, tugging her jeans down.

She didn't pull away. She leaned toward him, helping him lower them. Boots and pants came off in one smooth motion.

He covered her with his mouth again.

"Jeez."

He loved the word. The way she said it. There was surprise in her voice. And joy. But most of all, he heard longing.

"Jeez oh jeez oh jeez oh jeez."

He drew her panties down, heard her whimper. He tugged them lower, and when he had them off, urged her legs apart.

"Rand." But she didn't say his name in protest, she said it greedily.

He didn't need any prompting.

His mouth found her center. She opened for him. He sucked at her, and she cried out. Again. She moaned. The third time was her undoing, and he reveled in her release, the way her body tensed and then released again…and again.

"Oh, jeez," she moaned.

"That didn't take long," he teased.

"No," she gasped, still panting. "It didn't."

He stood up. "You're not afraid anymore, are you?"

Her pupils were still dilated with passion. "I don't know what I am."

"You've nothing to fear from me."

"I think that's what I'm afraid of."

Her honesty took him aback. But then again, Jessie always told the brutal truth. He knew that about her now. "Don't be afraid," he said. "Just enjoy."

He touched her, the evidence of her passion

warming his fingers. When he kissed her again, she didn't seem to mind the taste of herself, and he knew if he didn't have her soon he'd need to jump in the lake to cool off.

"Jessie," he panted, pressing against her.

Rand gasped when her hand found his erection.

"Yes," he urged, pushing into her.

She slid her hand beneath his waistband.

"Yes," he murmured.

Somehow his button popped free, then his zipper and then he was there, in her hand, moaning as she stroked him, her body sliding up his, her legs parting...

"Jessie," he said, "I don't have any protection."

"I don't care."

They should care. They should take it slow. But his body had a will of its own. He turned her, moving her toward a chaise lounge, backing her against it. She sank into the soft cushions.

"Are you sure?" he asked.

"I'm sure."

He covered her body with his. They kissed. His center found hers as if they'd done this a million times before. He slipped inside her.

She moaned.

When he withdrew from her, she followed him

with her hips. He thrust into her again. And then he was withdrawing and thrusting over and over again, as they kissed greedily.

"Rand," she gasped. "Ra-a-and."

He felt her come again, felt that sweet tightening that told him it was time for his own release. One stoke, two and then he cried out her name.

"Jessie," he said, kissing her lips, her chin, her cheeks. "Sweet Jessie."

Chapter Seventeen

Jessie came back to earth with a contented sigh, only to have the voice of reason intrude on her peace like an explosion.

What had they just done?

When he shifted, she stiffened, expecting to see the same panic on his face. Instead all she saw was tenderness.

"And to think I thought you were afraid of sex." She felt his chest vibrate a split second before she heard him chuckle. "Obviously, I was wrong."

"Rand, I—"

"Shh," he said. "I can see the buyer's remorse in your eyes."

The *what?*

"But it's going to be okay, Jessie." His hand came up to stroke her cheek. "We'll take it slow. We don't have to rush into anything."

"We already rushed into something," she couldn't help but point out.

"Don't worry. I'll be there for you if…something should come of…this."

He didn't say he'd marry her.

Jessie was shocked the thought would cross her mind. Rand and marriage.

"I know you'll do the right thing," she said to cover her surprise.

"Are you ready to eat?"

"I will be after I take a dip in that lake."

"Are you sure? It's cold."

Oh, she was sure. She dove into the water.

"Jessie!" She heard Rand call her name just before she sank beneath the surface.

In hindsight it probably wasn't the smartest thing to do. There might have been rocks nearby, or the bottom might not have been all that deep. But the ice-cold water did the trick, halting her spiraling thoughts.

She gasped for breath when her head broke the surface.

"Jeez, Jessie. I can't believe you did that."

"It feels good," she said, diving back under again.

"That water can't be more than sixty degrees," he said when she came up for air again.

It *felt* like sixty degrees.

"Here," he said, handing her one of the blankets from the boat when she pulled herself out.

"Thanks."

"You're shivering."

"I'm fine," she said.

"Come here."

Rand, dressed again, drew her into his arms. A spasm ripped through her body, although she wasn't all that certain it had to do with the chill of the lake.

"Better?" he asked.

"Better," she lied, wrapping the blanket around her. "And hungry," she added, telling herself everything would be just fine.

"Come on," he said. "Get dressed. I'll set up dinner."

"Great," she said.

"We better eat fast before my mom figures out what we've been up to."

Does it matter if she figures it out? Jessie wondered.

The Biddy Brigade had set the two of them up.

"Rand," she said, "If I wanted to go to dinner one night in town, would you take me?"

In the middle of pulling the basket out of the boat, he turned toward her. "What?"

"Are you worried about what people in town might say about us?"

He didn't respond for long, uncomfortable seconds. "Why the heck do you feel the need to ask that?"

She shrugged. "People will talk. I was just curious if it would bug you."

"Jessie, I don't care what anyone says about us." He squatted down in front of her, placing a hand on her shoulder. "I care about you, not other folks."

Then why had he said, "I'll take care of you," as if she'd be a kept woman?

"And to prove how serious I am, I'm going to take you to dinner Saturday night."

"Oh, yeah? Where?"

"At the town hall. The Chamber of Commerce organized a formal dinner and dance for local business owners. Everybody who's anybody will be there."

"I hadn't heard."

"You up to attending?" he asked.

Was she? Was she up to facing members of the community on Rand's arm? What would she do if they were rude to her? Or worse, Rand?

Stand up to them. Just as you always do.

"I'm up to it," she said firmly.

"Good." He bent down and kissed her. "Because

it's about time this town realized you're no longer Jessie the Jezebel."

A COUPLE DAYS LATER, Jessie still wasn't convinced attending the dinner was a good idea. She might put a brave face on things, but inwardly she was a cowardly mess.

She pulled back her family room curtain, searching for Rand's truck. At least she looked like a million bucks. The ankle-length gown with its crisscross bodice and flared skirt might be a bit formal, but she didn't care. The silky black fabric clung to her body like it had been made for her. Oddly enough, the color didn't wash her out, and she'd played up her bronze skin by darkening her eyes and highlighting her cheeks with rosy blush.

She heard a diesel truck, realized she'd been staring outside without even looking and dropped the curtain. It was Rand.

She didn't want him coming to the door, because he'd kiss her, and if he started to kiss her, she'd be powerless to resist him. Not to mention he'd ruin her makeup. She dashed out to meet him.

"Wow," he said.

"You like?" she asked, twirling in front of him.

"I like very much," he said in a low, husky voice.

He looked spectacular himself in the dusky evening light. He wore a business suit, but it was casual. Brown, button-down sport coat with a beige shirt underneath. The cowboy hat she'd only ever seen him without once—the first night they'd made love—was firmly atop his head. The tan slacks and polished brown cowboy boots looked perfect for Los Molinos society.

Suddenly, she felt overdressed.

"You ready?" he asked.

As I'll ever be. "Ready," she said brightly.

He looked at her strangely. She realized she had a death grip on the beaded black bag she'd picked up at the discount store along with the dress.

"You driving, or shall I?" It was a joke, because her poor car was really starting to show its age. Rand had promised to give her a raise just so she could go out and buy a new one. She wasn't sure if he'd been serious or not, but she felt like she deserved a raise after the hectic week they'd had at the clinic.

"You look nervous."

"Nervous? Me? Nah."

He caught up to her when she had her hand on his truck door. "I'll get that," he said. But when he didn't open it right away, she glanced up.

"You look beautiful," he said, bending and placing a kiss against her lips. "You're going to knock 'em dead."

Was she that transparent? Could he really see how much this night meant to her? All her life she'd felt like an outsider looking in. Life in a small town was that way. You had your upper crust and your lower crust…and then you had your rednecks.

And you've worked hard to put that life behind you.

But that didn't help to allay her fears. The whole way to the hall she fiddled with her purse, checked her makeup about ten thousand times and smoothed the skirt of her dress. A few times Rand opened his mouth as if to speak, but he never did. He must have figured this was something she had to work through on her own.

The dinner-dance was in the community center, which doubled as an indoor flea market on Sundays, the building on the outskirts of town. When they arrived, the sun had sunk beneath the horizon, leaving behind a pink glow that hovered over the low-lying mountains. The center was ablaze with lights when they pulled to a stop in front of the single-story building. Rumor had it Scott Berringer had landed his helicopter in the pasture next to the gravel parking lot. She would bet the billionaire rancher never had trouble fitting in.

Here we go.

The sound of music could be heard. Rand took her hand, and Jessie's heels sank into the ground as soon as she slid off her seat. Her legs felt wobbly, but that might be because of the shoes. Somehow she doubted it.

"Hey, Rand," someone called. Jim, the owner of the local feed store, came toward them, his pretty wife in tow. "Good to see you here," he said.

"Told you I'd come to one of these things sooner or later." The headlights of arriving cars swept over them. "You know Jessie, don't you?"

The glow from inside the building enabled Jessie to see the expression on Jim's face perfectly. "Hey, Jessie," he said. "Good to see you here, too."

Okay, so that wasn't the reaction she'd been expecting, although she wasn't sure exactly *what* she thought might happen. She'd never been openly shunned by anybody. Except maybe Martha. Well, all right, Jessie had overheard more than a few digs in her lifetime, but mostly from members of Rand's family and extended family—that was it. And so why she'd expected people to give her the cold shoulder, she had no idea.

It was the same inside the building. The hall had been transformed into a room as elegant as any hotel ballroom. White linens covered the large round tables, places set with crystal. Centerpieces with roses, lilies and mums scented the air.

"Rand...Jessie!"

Jessie smiled when she saw who was calling. Lani Cavenaugh came toward her, a huge grin on her pretty face. "Wow," she said, leaning back after giving Jessie a hug. "Look at you."

"Is it too fancy?" Jessie asked. "I feel over-dressed."

"Are you kidding? You look stunning."

"Where's that no-good husband of yours?" Rand asked, coming up behind Jessie.

"He's over there talking to Scott."

Scott? As in Scott Berringer? Jessie had seen the billionaire around town, but never up close.

"Come on," Lani said. "I'll introduce you. You know Amanda, don't you?"

She did. They'd gone to school together, but the two of them had never been friendly. Amanda had made it clear she didn't approve of the party crowd.

Jessie tensed as they were introduced.

She needn't have worried.

Amanda and her husband were so nice and so welcoming, Jessie felt immediately at ease.

"So, how's Nick?" Scott asked, his blue eyes sweeping the crowd. He was one of the few men in the room who'd refrained from wearing a cowboy hat, probably a good thing. His hair was so wavy.

"Happy as a clam," Rand said. "He'd always wanted to immerse himself in research. This new medical facility of his is right up his alley."

"And how's Caroline? Is your sister still in contention to make the NFR?"

"Of course," Rand said. "Although we'd all be happier with her at home."

"I'm not surprised. You've never made a secret of your views of women in the workforce," Amanda said, something that gave Jessie pause. Rand wasn't the caveman type.

Was he?

"Okay, everyone," an officious woman called. "Time to take your seats."

"Do we all want to sit together?" Lani asked.

"Sure," Jessie answered. Amanda had to be mistaken. After all, Rand had hired her to be his assistant. Obviously, he didn't have a problem with women working.

"After you," he said, offering her his arm.

Jessie found herself sitting at a table with the *crème de la crème* of Los Molinos society.

What a strange world.

But as the dinner progressed, she came to realize that maybe, just maybe, it'd all been in her head. Maybe she really wasn't the pariah she'd thought she was all these years.

The dinner turned out to be a community fundraiser. Items donated by business owners present were auctioned off, including free pet examinations from Rand. Jessie couldn't believe it when, after dinner was over, Rand handed her a paddle and told her to bid on whatever she wanted. When a brown suede jacket with genuine sheepskin lining came up for bid, she found herself tempted, but just couldn't bring herself to spend someone else's money. Rand solved the problem by taking the paddle from her.

"Here," he said, lifting it.

"Rand," she whispered, "I don't need that."

He looked at her incredulously. "Are you kidding? That jacket you wear to work is about to fall apart."

"But *I* want the jacket," Lani said from across the table.

"Uh-oh," Chase said.

A bidding war ensued that would no doubt be the talk of the town the next morning. The jacket likely sold for more than triple its actual price, and in the end Jessie suspected Lani gave it up so that she could have it. The place erupted into applause when Rand won. Jessie had to stand up and try the jacket on—a perfect fit—which elicited more applause.

She felt like crying.

If someone had told her she'd be participating in a community service event, one where the townspeople would actually applaud her, she'd have thought that person nuts. And yet here she was.

"Do you like it?" Rand asked as she sat back down.

"Are you kidding? I'm never taking it off," she said, knowing the smile on her face must be a thousand watts.

"That might present a bit of a problem later tonight."

She blushed. Jessie knew he could tell when he laughed. She cocked a brow and leaned in close. "Oh, that won't be a problem," she said. "I've always wanted to make love wearing nothing but a fur-lined jacket."

Rand's smile faded. Jessie's face heated up even

more. Her heart did something funny, too, something that made her sit up straighter.

Rand lifted a hand. "Check, please!"

Chapter Eighteen

They almost didn't make it to his truck. Rand pulled her off to the side of the building the moment they got outdoors, and kissed her.

She kissed him back. As his hand slipped beneath her new jacket and cupped her breast, Jessie moaned. He took advantage of her open mouth and thrust his tongue inside. Rand groaned in delight when she did the same.

"Jeez," she said, pulling back for air a few minutes later.

"Jeez is right. If I'd known buying you a jacket would cause this reaction, I'd have bought you one a long time ago."

Inside the building the auctioneer's rhythmic call was followed by applause.

"Come on," Rand said. "Let's get out of here."

"Where are we going?" she inquired.

"To my house."

She stopped.

"What?" he asked.

"I've never been to your house before."

"So?"

"So, I just thought…"

He watched as she struggled for words. Earlier, he'd seen the tears in her eyes when he'd bought her the coat, but it was now, as he stared down at her, that he realized what was wrong.

"You thought I'd take you to a hotel or something? That I didn't consider you good enough to bring home?"

"No, that's not it."

He framed her legs with his and tilted her face up. "Jessie, when are you going to learn I'm not ashamed of you? That I'm proud to have you on my arm?"

"That's not it," she said with a shake of her head. "I was just going to say that I never thought I'd be lucky enough to be with you, and that I'm grateful, so grateful—"

He kissed her, humbled by her words. *He* was the one who was lucky. She'd given him a second chance. She had a tremendous capacity to forgive. It was one of the things he cherished about her.

He took her to his house. His home was on the outskirts of town in a single-story ranch house with a nice front porch. Nothing fancy. Jessie looked around her like it was a castle.

"Can I take your coat?" he asked in the entry hall.

"No," she said, giving him a tremulous smile. "I told you what I want to do with this coat."

The erection he had, already straining against the crotch of his pants, suddenly got harder.

"Then why don't you go change while I put on some music? My bedroom's past the kitchen, down the hall."

She nodded. Rand's hands were shaking as he selected a few CDs.

He felt like a man on his honeymoon.

And maybe in some ways he was. This was a first for him. The first time he'd ever brought a woman home. Jessie might have a hard time believing that, but the truth of the matter was he'd never been one to play around much. If a woman interested him they went back to her place. That was the way it worked, although one or two hadn't liked it.

"Ready?" he called.

Jessie didn't answer.

Rand rubbed his palms against his slacks. He

flipped on the light switch in the family room as he passed, wondering if Jessie liked the western-style motif he'd used in decorating the house.

"Jessie?" He flipped on the hall light, paused inside his doorway.

She lay on the bed, the jacket open, nothing on beneath.

"Oh, Jessie." Nothing, absolutely nothing and nobody had ever looked so beautiful.

"Well, are you going to stand there all day, or are you going to join me?"

He undid his belt. Slowly, he pulled it from the loops.

Her eyes burned him.

Next he undid his pants, dropping them to the floor. His shirt and boxers came next. His hat he flung into a corner.

When their bodies touched, Rand gasped at how good it felt to be with her. They'd worked together for nearly two weeks now, and each day Rand marveled at how incredibly special she was. She gave herself wholeheartedly to everything—to him, their patients, even Pauline. Her generous nature and loving touch stirred him like no other woman before.

"Rand," she said softly.

He shifted her beneath him. "Jessie, darling Jessie," he murmured, and then kissed her.

Her mouth was soft and yet firm—as if the strength of her personality ran through her body to his. When he slowly slid into her, their connection became even more pronounced.

And as he had the first time they made love, he drew back and looked into her eyes. He decided that he loved watching her as he moved in and out, loved to watch her eyes grow unfocused, her face tense and then slacken the higher she climbed.

"Rand," she cried out again.

Her eyes widened, her body tensed. He slid her hands up above her head, all the while watching. She was about to climax. He wanted her to. God, he wanted to please her.

She threw her head back, and when her body tightened around him, he lost the battle for control.

A long time later, they slid back to earth.

"Jessie," he murmured softly.

"I think I'm falling in love with you," she said.

"I think I'm falling in love with you, too," he answered, and they kissed—the kiss of two people who'd found each other at last. As Rand held her tightly, he had a feeling Jessie would be the only woman he'd ever love.

He courted her.

It was an old-fashioned word, but to Jessie it was the only way to describe the next few weeks.

At work Rand was solicitous and professional, although not above stealing the odd kiss. Her days were filled with work and her nights filled with passion, and if sometimes she woke up in Rand's arms with her heart pounding, she told herself that was okay. She was just new to this whole love thing, so naturally it felt strange.

Nobody in town said a word about their dating. Then again, why would they? She'd been wrong, she realized. Not everyone hated her. Word had spread about Tommy. She had Rand to thank for that. Oh, there was little doubt that a *few* people didn't like her much, but that was just Tommy's family.

Rand's family accepted her with open arms. Caroline was still out on the rodeo trail, but everyone had assured Jessie she'd be home soon. Jessie couldn't wait to meet the barrel racing star.

But she did meet Rand's brother, Nick, who popped into the ranch with his new wife, Alison—or Ali, as she liked to be called. Jessie had known Rand's brother was a surgeon, but she'd had no idea that he specialized in reconstructive surgery for burn victims.

"You ready to go on a ride?" Rand asked after they'd shared a family dinner at the ranch.

"Ready," she said with a glance around the table. She would realize later that there'd been something strange in the faces of her dining companions, but at the moment she was too focused on riding to notice. It'd been forever since she'd last been on the back of a horse.

"Have fun," Rand's mother said.

"We will." Jessie was so excited, she felt as if she couldn't be happier. But along with that happiness came the ever-present niggling doubts. How many times had she been at a point in her life where things had been going great, only to have everything suddenly come crashing down?

"What are you thinking?" Rand asked as they walked toward the stables. It was early summer and the days were getting longer and longer—something Jessie usually enjoyed.

She knew he'd tell her she was worried about nothing, so she just smiled. "About how happy I am."

"Good," he said, pulling her up against him beneath one of the large oaks. Sunlight dappled their bodies. She rested her head on his shoulder. She was being foolish. What could possibly happen?

Rand was a great man. She doubted he'd have any skeletons in his closet. And so, what was it?

Nothing, she decided, determined to enjoy the rest of the day. They had a few more hours of sunlight, and she would spend them on horseback.

"You know, we really should get you your own horse."

"You think?" she asked, looking up quickly and blinking against the sun.

Beneath his tan cowboy hat, Rand's expression told her he was as happy as she was. "Sure," he said. "We could keep it out here. Lots of room to ride, and my mom has ranch hands who'll muck out the horse's stall."

"Who says I don't want to muck out my own stalls?"

"Do you?"

"Of course," she said. "That's part of owning a horse."

"You only say that because you haven't owned one before."

"And you only say *that* because you're jaded and spoiled where horses are concerned."

"No, I'm not."

"Yes, you are," she teased. "You've had horses all

your life, while I've only ever dreamed about them. It's why I wanted to work with large animals."

"I know," he said, and there was approval in his voice. "And you should be proud of what you've accomplished."

"I am," she said softly.

"What color horse would you like?" He questioned her while they walked down the dirt path. Color, size, breed—he wanted to know it all. Jessie suspected she might find a horse in her stocking one day soon.

In the barn, they stopped and said hello to Peanut, who'd made a full recovery. The pony nickered softly, and Jessie was sorry she hadn't brought any treats.

Rand helped her to saddle up, something Jessie had done only a few times before. Fortunately, it was a lot easier to put a bridle on a horse than a saddle. Lighter, too.

And then they led their mounts outdoors.

Her heart pounded as if she were standing at the bottom of a mountain, which, she thought as she eyed the black-and-white paint in front of her, she kind of was.

"Here, let me give you a leg up," Rand said.

"No, thanks," Jessie answered. "I can do this on

my own." She'd ridden a few times before and knew it wasn't hard.

"You sure?"

Grabbing the reins in one hand and the stirrup in the other, Jessie half climbed, half pulled herself up, every muscle in her body protesting as she did so.

"Well done," Rand said, mounting his own chestnut gelding.

"Just wait until you see me gallop."

"No galloping," he said sternly.

"Why not?"

"Because it's been a while since you've ridden, and with my luck you'll fall off and break your pretty little neck, and then what would I do?"

"Hire a new vet tech."

He frowned, but the straight line of his lips quickly turned up, and he chuckled. "I guess I would. But I'll probably have to do that soon, anyway."

"Oh, yeah? Why?"

He didn't answer, just clucked to make his horse move forward.

"Hey," she protested. It hurt to trot.

"Come on," he called. "If you can keep up, I'll let you gallop."

One thing about riding a horse—once you knew

how, you never forgot. Jessie spurred her horse, the obedient paint pricking his ears before lurching into a canter.

"Last one to the lake is a rotten egg," she yelled as she passed Rand.

"Hey!"

They galloped down the tree-studded path, and by the time they reached the lake, Rand was in the lead. He turned along the shoreline and soon they'd left the guest cabins behind.

"Wow," Jessie said when they pulled their horses to a stop on top of a small knoll. "That was fun."

"This is one of my favorite trails."

"Where does it lead?"

"To the top of that ridge over there," he said, indicating with his chin.

"That far?"

"You up for it?"

"Baby, I was born to ride," she said.

It took them a while, and Jessie had a feeling she'd be too sore to walk tomorrow. But it was worth it, she decided, when they finally reached the summit of what seemed to her a mountain at the end of the trail. She had never seen a prettier view of Los Molinos.

In the valley beneath, far in the distance, tiny

cars were driving up and down Main Street. On the edge of town she could see the alfalfa fields, green pastures that were a stark contrast to the dried brown grass covering the hillsides this time of year.

"Is that the clinic?" she asked, pointing.

"It is," he said. "And there's Route 49. You can see where it merges with 580 over there."

"Look at that."

They fell into silence, Jessie so engrossed in the view that she didn't even see Rand climb down.

"Beautiful," he said.

"Yes, it is."

When she glanced down at him she realized he was talking about her.

"Oh, uh, thanks," she said.

He led his horse forward until he was standing beside her. "You are beautiful, Jessie. More beautiful than any woman I've ever known," he said, staring up at her.

"Aw. I bet you say that to all the girls."

"No, just one," he said, getting down on one knee.

"What are you doing?"

"What do you think?"

"You look like—" The breath left her.

He pulled a small black box from his pocket.

"Oh. My. Gosh."

"Jessie," he said softly. "Will you marry me?"

Chapter Nineteen

Rand watched as she covered her cheeks with her hands, her eyes darting between him and the ring, him and the ring.

"Will you?" he asked again, starting to get nervous.

She slid off her horse, all the while looking stunned. And confused. And maybe even scared.

And then he heard it, the word barely a whisper.
"Yes."

He shot up, startling her horse. He didn't care. Because he had her in his arms and he was never letting her go. "I thought for a moment you were going to say no," he said.

"I couldn't believe it," she said, gasping for a breath. "I've been hoping you would ask me. Come to think of it, what took you so long?"

"I had to find the perfect ring." He opened the black box, exposing a flawless white diamond ring on a bed of red velvet.

"Oh, Rand," she whispered. "It's stunning."

"It is," he said, slipping it on her finger. "Just like you."

"And *huge*." She giggled.

"Like certain parts of *me*."

"Rand." She playfully hit him on the shoulder and then fell into his arms again, suddenly crying and laughing. Rand felt better. He'd done it. And she'd said yes.

Thank God.

"Pauline's going to freak out," he heard her mumble.

"Why do you say that?" he asked, leaning back. "She's been fine about us."

"She *tolerated* us dating. She won't like that I'm marrying the boss."

"Yeah, well," he said with a soft smile, "you'll be pregnant soon and so she won't be working with you for all that long."

"Even if I did get pregnant right away, it wouldn't stop me from working at the clinic."

"You can't work while you're pregnant."

"Yes, I can."

He lifted his eyebrows. "Jessie, don't be silly. It'd be too dangerous."

"I could work through my second trimester. Female vets do it all the time."

"Those are *small*-animal vets."

"Well, who says I'm getting pregnant right away?"

"Don't you want to have kids?"

"Of course I do, but not until I finish vet school."

"What?"

He thought he'd misheard her, had to draw back and watch her mouth move as she said, "I was thinking of going to vet school."

"But...why?"

"Because I'm good at this, Rand," she said, crossing her arms in front of her. "And I got good grades in school. It took me a while to finish my course, but I aced the classes. So I've been thinking lately of applying to UC Davis. It's only a couple hours away. And if I schedule the classes right, I'd still be able to work part-time so I could pay for it."

"You want to become a vet?" He had to ask again because he just couldn't believe he was hearing this...now.

"Well, yeah," she admitted. "I've been thinking about it. But it doesn't have to change anything."

"But what about starting a family?"

"Hey. These eggs aren't going anywhere," she said, trying to draw a smile from him. "We can wait a few years."

"But if you get accepted to vet school you'll be gone a lot. I'll have to hire someone to take your place."

"I can help you do that. Especially now that I know your needs," she said with a smile, lifting her hand—the diamond catching the light—and pushing a strand of his hair back under his cowboy hat.

He leaned away.

"Whoa," she said, her mouth dropping open. "What's the matter?"

"You should have told me this before."

"Why? Would it have changed your mind about us?"

He didn't say anything.

"C'mon, Rand. You're not telling me you expected me to marry you, go home and start raising babies."

"No. I didn't expect that," he said. His horse snorted, distracting her. "At least not right away." He turned, lifting his hat and running a hand through his hair.

"What's that supposed to mean?"

He thought about it for a moment, his eyes scanning the valley below. "I wasn't expecting this, that's all."

"So you did expect me to quit work and raise babies."

He shrugged. "I guess I did."

"I don't want to do that, Rand." She twisted the reins in her hand.

"Then I guess that's that."

"You make it sound as if my wanting a career is a bad thing."

He shook his head. "Look, I'm not going to pretend I'm not disappointed. I thought we were on the same page. That you'd want to start a family sooner rather than later. I was wrong." He shrugged. "I'll deal with it."

"And if I *don't* want kids?" she asked, stroking her horse's neck absently.

His brows lifted.

"If I decide I'd rather have a career than a family? What then?"

"That's not what you're saying, though."

"It might be," she said. "I have no idea what I'll want to do in a few years. But if having a family is important to you, Rand, tell me now because I'm telling *you* now that I might not want one."

"Jessie, let's talk about this later. You sound like you're getting angry, and there's no reason. My point is only that I think we should talk more about this before making any big decisions. C'mon," he said. "Let's head back to the ranch. I don't want to get caught out here in the dark."

And she noticed he didn't offer her any reassurances. In fact, he didn't say anything the whole ride home. Jessie eyed the sparkling new diamond on her finger and wondered if she'd made a mistake.

And what would she do if she *had?*

"CONGRATULATIONS!" A chorus of voices rang out the moment Rand walked through the door.

He paused in the doorway, alone.

"Where's Jessie?" his mom asked. The high-backed chair she sat in made it appear as if she sat on a throne. Ali and Nick sat on the sofa to her right.

"Went home."

"What?" Ali asked. "Did she say no?"

"She said yes." Rand looked around the private family drawing room. He was glad they were away from the guests.

"Then why'd she go home?" Nick asked. "I was hoping to say goodbye to my new future sister-in-law. We're leaving for Texas tomorrow."

"She's upset," Rand admitted, taking his hat off as he sat down. He tossed it on the side table next to him, stretching his legs out.

"What's she upset about?" his mother asked. She was dressed in her owner-of-the-guest-ranch clothes, which meant she was more dressed up than usual in a fifties-style western shirt and denim skirt.

"She doesn't want kids."

"What?"

He'd known that would get her attention. His mom's main reason for marrying off her sons was so she could have grandchildren. Now that Jessie didn't appear to want any, it would be a black mark against her.

"She told you she didn't want kids?"

"No, she didn't say that exactly. But it's something she wants me to consider as a possibility."

"And you told her that wasn't acceptable," Nick said, his voice disapproving.

"I didn't say that," he said. "I was disappointed, but I told her we should probably talk about it more."

"No kids," his mom murmured, the fixture above her head casting soft light on her gray hair. "I would have never guessed that about her."

"Maybe you should have checked her hips like you did mine," Ali said, leaning forward and tossing the magazine she'd been studying on the coffee table in front of her.

"I never checked your hips," Martha protested. "It was you who offered to show me your teeth."

Ali chuckled, but her amusement faded when Rand didn't laugh. "Cheer up, Rand. From what you've told me about her, she's fiercely independent. And she just graduated from college. I'm not surprised she doesn't want kids right now."

"She may not want them *ever.*"

"And will that be a problem?" asked his brother, arms resting on his knees, staring at him intently.

"I don't know," he answered, running a hand through his hair. Dust rose from his jeans when he set his hand down on his leg. "It might."

"Oh, that's right," Ali said. "You Sheppard men are into reproducing."

"Not necessarily," Rand answered. "I don't know. I just always assumed I'd have kids."

"And you still might," his mom said. "She didn't say no, Rand. Get a wedding ring on that finger of hers. She'll come around."

"But what if she doesn't?" asked Nick, the pragmatist.

What if she didn't?

Chapter Twenty

Things had changed between them.

Jessie would have been a fool not to notice the tension. Several times that first day she felt tempted to take the ring off and hand it back to him.

It wasn't so much that he acted uptight or even mad. It was other things. When a canine patient came in and tried to snap at her, Rand stepped in, telling her to stand back while he stitched the dog up. It wasn't her job to stand back, and she resented being told to.

Things finally came to a head when they were forced to deal with a surly horse.

"What's with our patients today?" Jessie asked, grasping the lead rope as they stood in the barn aisle. "They're all trying to take our heads off."

"Just hold on tight," Rand said, eyeing the big chestnut, whose ears were pinned back flat.

"He doesn't look happy," said Debra, the horse's owner, a middle-aged brunette woman who didn't look fit enough to ride.

"He just doesn't like me poking around," Rand said, palpating the horse's belly. Judging by the swelling, Jessie was pretty certain the animal had an infection.

"Well, Debra," Rand said. "It feels like an abscess. There's no granular discharge usually associated with pigeon fever. But we should probably do a culture just to be—Jessie!"

Jessie turned right as the gelding's teeth sank into her arm.

Holy—

"Oh my gosh! Are you all right?" Debra gasped.

"Fine," Jessie managed to mutter. The horse's teeth had left a rip in the fabric of her long-sleeved shirt.

"Damn it, Jessie. I told you to watch it."

"Here, let me take him," Debra said.

"No, no. That's okay."

"It's not okay," Rand said. "Does he cross tie?"

"He does."

"It's *fine*," Jessie said. "Honestly, it's just a pinch."

A pinch that throbbed. And she could feel a hematoma sprouting already.

"Jessie—"

"Rand, this poor horse needs attention. I'll be fine."

He didn't look convinced.

"I can always bring him back later," Debra said.

"No, no," Rand answered, studying Jessie closely. "Are you sure?"

"I'm sure," she said with a smile that she hoped concealed the pain.

He went back to work. Jessie clenched her teeth, and when it came time to lead the horse to the exam room, gasped when the horse jerked his head.

She bit her lip throughout the rest of the procedure and smiled at Debra again when they finally finished up. "He'll likely be good as new in a few days," she said.

"Make sure you keep up his antibiotics," Rand advised. "We'll have the results of his culture in a few days."

"Thanks, Doctor," the woman said, leading the horse away.

"Jessie, come here."

"Can it wait a minute?" she asked. "I want to clean up the exam room."

"No, it can't." Rand placed a hand on her

shoulder and led her toward the surgical room. "We're going to have a look at that arm."

"It's fine."

"It's *not* fine," he said, stopping in front of the sink. There were no windows inside the room but the fluorescent lights above them illuminated the concern on his face. "You're in considerable pain. I can see that."

Not even Jessie expected the nasty sight revealed when he unbuttoned her cuff and gently rolled up the sleeve.

"Oh, jeez," she said. The skin below the shoulder was broken and a bruised area had already swelled to the size of a fist.

He met her gaze. "Why the hell didn't you tell me you were hurt this bad?"

"Because I'm *not* hurt badly. It's just a bruise. It'll go away in a couple of days."

"And in the meantime you can't use that arm."

"Yes, I can. See?" She tried to lift it, but couldn't.

"Damn it," he said, stepping back. "I told you to watch yourself."

"I thought I was far enough away."

"You weren't."

"Obviously."

"Let's put some ice on it," he said, turning toward the cold storage unit in the corner of the room.

"I just need to keep using it. If I stop moving it'll freeze up on me."

"Maybe you should go home. You shouldn't work with your arm like that."

"My arm is fine," she repeated. She rested her back against the counter, studying him. "What's really at issue here?"

"What are you talking about?"

"You've been acting weird all day, even before I was bitten." She tilted her head to the side. He'd stopped in front of her, ice in hand. "You weren't like this until you asked me to marry you."

"I care about you, Jessie. What do you expect me to do? Watch you get hurt?" He handed her the ice.

She pressed it against her arm, wincing. "This is my job, and I expect you to let me *do* it. I'm not going to get hurt."

"You just did."

"Minor. It'll be good as new in a day or two," she said with a wave of her free hand. But the movement caused her to bite back a gasp.

"I don't like it when you're hurt. It makes me angry. Not at you, but at myself for not protecting you better."

"You can't *always* protect me, Rand."

"I can try."

"Not if we're going to make this work. You have to let me make my own choices."

He held her gaze. "This isn't about your arm, is it?" he asked.

Wasn't it? She didn't know. Ever since his proposal she'd been edgy. Last night she'd tossed and turned, the disquiet she'd felt on and off since they'd started dating returning tenfold.

She was scared.

"Rand, I—"

"Don't say it. I can see it in your eyes. You're terrified, Jessie."

"I'm not scared," she lied, placing the ice pack next to the sink. It was too cold. "I'm just…apprehensive."

"If you loved me, you wouldn't be apprehensive at all."

"I do love you," she said, moving closer. "I do love you. More than any other person I've ever known."

"But is that enough to marry me? Because I've got to be honest, when I proposed to you last night I expected you to fly into my arms."

"I did," she said, lifting her good arm to clasp his hand.

"For a split second you looked ready to gallop off in the other direction. And then when we got back to the ranch, instead of coming in and celebrating with my family, you spouted some nonsense about needing to get home."

"I was tired."

"You were scared," he said, squeezing her fingers. "You're still scared."

"No, I'm not, Rand. I'm just concerned about a few things...like having children and my going back to vet school. Marriage is such a big step. And it involves a lot of big decisions."

"They won't be big decisions if you say yes to the right man."

"You are the right man," she said, clutching his arm. "Of course you are."

"If you really wanted to marry me you wouldn't be afraid of the future. You'd know that I'm going to be here for you, whatever choices you make."

Nobody had ever been there for her before, not even her mother, who lived five minutes away.

"I love you, Rand."

"All this time," he said softly, lifting his hand to her cheek. "All this time you've been on your own. You've put yourself through school, gotten your degree, found a job—on your own. Suddenly I come along and I want it all. I want your heart, your soul, and most importantly, want to be part of the life you've carved out for yourself."

"We'll make a new life…"

He stroked her cheek with his thumb, and Jessie wanted to close her eyes, absorb the comfort. Except she couldn't. Her heart was beating too fast. Only this time she put a name to her anxiety. It wasn't really anxiety—more a feeling of suffocation.

Chapter Twenty-One

Rand watched as the emotions crossed her face. "You finally understand what I'm trying to say, don't you?" he murmured

She nodded. "I think I do."

He dropped his hand to his side. "You don't have to give the ring back."

She glanced down as if she'd forgotten about it. Outside the dogs in the kennel had started to bark, a sure sign that another client had pulled up.

"Rand, I—"

"Shh," he soothed, and at that moment he realized he didn't need to have children. His world would be complete if he just had Jessie. "You don't need to explain. I understand."

Tears shimmered at the edge of her lashes, making her eyes look huge. "I'm sorry, Rand."

"I am, too."

"I love you."

"I know," he said. "I love you, too."

"Can't we try to live together first?"

He smiled, but it was a halfhearted attempt. "You want to try me on before buying?"

"Something like that."

He shook his head. "It's all or nothing for me, Jess."

She nodded, and his heart sank as he saw her slip the ring off her finger. "You should keep this," she said.

"You know where it'll be."

"I know."

He pulled her to him, careful of her injured arm. She seemed to melt into his embrace. He heard her sniff.

"Take care of yourself, Jessie," he said, stepping back.

"Do you want me to…I mean, do you think we should still work together?" she asked, wiping away tear tracks.

"What do you think?"

She looked so sad again. "Probably not."

"No," he echoed. "Probably not."

"I have a friend, someone I met in vet tech school. She might be able to fill in."

"Give me her number."

Jessie nodded, writing it down on a piece of paper. "I'll call her today," he said when she handed it to him.

"I can stay—"

"No," he said. "Go home and rest your arm. You never know when you might need it for some other horse to snack on."

She smiled, but he could tell it was forced. "Thanks."

That sounded an awful lot like goodbye. But surely once she realized what they'd had, she'd be back.

"I'll get a reference letter to Pauline by the end of the day."

Jessie stretched up and kissed him. "I'll call you," she said.

But as he watched her walk away, he wondered who was fooling whom.

COWARD. Fool. Idiot.

Jessie called herself all those things and more as she drove home.

What was the matter with her?

She stared at the spot where the ring had been. Even though it'd only been on her finger a short time, there was already a dent.

You chickened out.

She couldn't forget the burst of relief she'd felt when Rand had let her off the hook.

"Damn it," she muttered as she locked her car door. She should have gone off and eloped. That would have prevented her from having cold feet.

"Hello, Jessie."

Jessie yelped as Tommy appeared out of nowhere.

"T-Tommy. You startled me."

"Heard you and my cousin got engaged."

"Yeah. Go figure," she said, eyeing the door to her apartment complex. Suddenly, it seemed far away.

"Congratulations."

But the look on his face wasn't friendly. "Thanks," she said. "Um, I've got to get inside. Big date tonight, you know."

"You let me go to jail," he said as she turned.

She spun to face him, incredulous. "Excuse me?"

"And now you've *really* done it. My dad's kicked me out. Doesn't even want me working for him. I've got nothing."

He'd been drinking. She could smell it on her breath. "Gee, I'm sorry, Tommy." She looked around, hoping to see a pedestrian on the street, or someone driving up. No luck. "Next time I'll be certain to take the blame for something I didn't do. Oh, and keep covering for you seven years later."

"I've been thinking," he said, almost as if he hadn't heard her. "You know, you really kind of owe me."

There was a look in his eyes, one she recognized.

He was strung out.

"Look, Tommy—"

He charged. She darted left. He caught her around the waist.

"Help!" she screamed.

Tommy's hand snaked over her mouth. She thrust an elbow into him, but this wasn't the same kid she'd fought off years ago.

"Let…me…go."

He flipped her around, their legs entangled. She hit the ground. Hard.

Jessie's vision blurred. Her cheek throbbed. Hands slipped beneath her armpits and started to drag her away. She twisted around, somehow got a leg up and jammed her heel into his thigh.

"Son of a—"

He let her go, and Jessie leaped to her feet and ran.

Right into the path of an oncoming car.

She saw it before it hit, tried to reverse direction. Too late. She heard a thud, knew it was the car striking her, and then…nothing.

"WHAT THE HELL HAPPENED?" Rand asked, his heart pounding nearly as hard as his feet as he ran down the hospital corridor.

His uncle shot up from his seat, the look on his face grave. "Rand, wait."

Rand charged up to the information desk. "I'm not going to wait."

"Rand," Uncle Phil said, managing to step in front of him. "I know where she is."

"I need Jessie Munroe's room number," he told the receptionist, an older woman with a kind expression and startling white hair.

"Munroe," she said calmly, no doubt used to concerned loved ones charging up to her in a panic.

"Rand, hold on. I know what room she's in."

The receptionist paused, looking at the two of them.

"She's in ICU," Phil said.

"Mother of—"

"That's right behind the elevators here, around the corner," Phil continued.

Rand was on his way before he could say another word.

"Rand, stop," his uncle ordered, grabbing his arm.

It was quiet in the ground-floor reception area. Jessie was in there fighting for her life, and yet this place was as quiet as a damn—

He couldn't finish the thought.

"Before you go in there," his uncle was saying, "I want you to know how sorry I am."

Rand tried to move on.

"No, wait." Phil pressed a hand in the middle of Rand's chest. "Please. When she wakes up, tell her how sorry the family is. Tell her when the cops called, I told them to do what they wanted with—" his voice broke "—with my son. I came down here straight away."

Rand finally paused long enough to see the fear and sorrow in his uncle's eyes. "This isn't your fault, Uncle Phil," he said, clasping the man's shoulder. It was his.

"It is," Phil said, wiping his eyes quickly. "I should have listened to you. Twice you tried to tell me what my son was like and both times I dismissed it."

And Rand should never have let Jessie walk out of the clinic....

Damn it.

His own eyes filled with tears. "I'll let her know," he said, moving on.

This time his uncle let him go.

When he found the ICU nursing station Rand had a hard time keeping it together. There were no glass-walled rooms he could look in to see if Jessie was all right. Where was she?

The nurse on duty must have seen the look in his eyes, because she immediately called a doctor over. "Rand Sheppard?" The man in the long white coat held out his hand. "I'm Mark Jones."

Rand didn't want to take it. He didn't want to stand there. He just wanted to see Jessie.

"Can you take me to Jessie Munroe's room?"

"I'm afraid not," Dr. Jones said. "At least not yet." He gently guided Rand away from the reception desk.

"We've done a CAT scan and found some swelling of the brain. We're trying to determine if we need to perform surgery right now—"

"Can I please see her?"

"No. Not while we're still running tests. You'd only be in the way."

"Rand?"

He turned, his control slipping even more when he saw his mother.

"Mom," he gasped.

"Nick's on his way," she said, pulling Rand into her embrace. She was a good foot and a half shorter than him, but her hug was Herculean. "I caught him at the airport."

"She's in ICU," Rand said. "They won't let me see her."

"I heard," Martha said in a low voice, holding him tight and rubbing his back. "We'll sit here and wait."

And he cried.

Chapter Twenty-Two

The low hum of voices woke Rand from his nap, a nap he hadn't even meant to take. He sat up, eyes blurry. What time was it?

His neck hurt from the way he'd been leaning against the wall.

Nick and their mom stood near the reception desk, talking with the doctor.

Rand shot up from his seat as the doctor turned and left. "What is it?" he asked. "What's going on?"

"Calm down," Nick said.

His brother had arrived a few hours after his mother, Ali was somewhere, Rand thought, looking around. What the hell time was it, anyway? "What's happening?" he asked. "Is she okay?"

"She's hanging in," Nick said, placing a hand on his shoulder. "The bad news is she's still in intensive care. The good news is they don't think she'll need surgery."

"Can I see her?" he asked.

"Yes, you can go in—"

Thank God.

"But, Rand," Nick said softly, "it's not pretty."

"You've seen her?"

He nodded. "The doctor gave me privileges once he heard my credentials. I've looked at her chart."

"And?"

"She's hurt, Rand. Bad. I'm not going to sugarcoat it."

Oh, God. He knew Nick wouldn't lie to him. The fact that he wasn't telling him everything would be all right meant...

"Where is she?"

"Room six."

Rand nodded, already moving. The place seemed deserted, the rooms sterile with their light brown linoleum floors and off-white walls.

The door to room six was open.

He slipped inside. The sight of Jessie, her head bandaged, her body hooked up to various machines and monitors, was almost more than he could take.

She was on a ventilator, the noise of the thing

nearly drowning out the beep-beep-beep of the heart monitor to her left. She looked like a battered rag doll.

"Oh, Jessie," he said softly.

He pulled a chair away from the wall, took her hand and simply held it. Her pale skin looked almost blue beneath the fluorescent lights.

"She'll make it."

Rand jumped.

In the corner of the room, by the door, sat a diminutive woman, her face nearly as pale as Jessie's.

"She's a fighter, that girl. Gave me twelve hours of hell when she came into the world. She'll make it."

Jessie's mother.

He could see the resemblance—faintly. This woman's face was worn, her brow furrowed into a permanent frown. Her faded red hair, cropped close to her head, might have been the same shade as Jessie's once. Or maybe not. It was hard to tell. But her eyes were the same.

"You must be Rand."

"I am."

He didn't get up, didn't let go of Jessie's hand.

"I'm Carolyn Munroe."

He'd never heard Jessie mention the name.

Never once talk about her mother. In hindsight, that seemed strange.

"I didn't know you were here."

"I saw your family when I came in, but I didn't introduce myself. Figured we'd all meet sooner or later." She had the crackly voice of a smoker. "She told me she was dating you."

Had she? Rand wondered, looking back at Jessie. A strand of red hair peeked out from beneath her bandages. He wanted to smooth it back, but was afraid to.

"I told her, 'honey'—" her voice cracked. "I said, 'honey, you better snap that one up.'"

"Oh?" Rand wasn't really listening. All he cared about was the steady beep of the heart monitor.

"But she didn't hear me. Probably would have broke up with you just like all the others."

What others?

"Can't keep a man around to save her life," her mother said, shaking her head.

It was dark outside. There was a small window beyond all the machinery, the glow from the lights turning the glass a reflective gray.

"I'm sure that's my fault," Jessie's mom confessed. "I could never keep a man around myself."

A nurse came in, smiled at them in the vague,

harried way hospital staff had. She checked the IV drip then left.

Rand had to search his mind to remember what Mrs. Monroe had been saying before the nurse came in. He needn't have worried. Carolyn picked up right where she'd left off.

"She's had a crush on you for ages."

"She has?"

The woman nodded. "Yup. Since tenth grade. You were already out of school, but I used to watch her eyes follow you whenever we'd see you in town. You were already off to vet school, and all Jessie would talk about was how she wanted to do that one day, too. 'Course, she couldn't. No money."

Rand's gaze shifted back to Jessie again. So stubborn. So damned determined. And now look.

"But she went and did it anyway," her mom said. "I didn't think she could, especially out living on her own like she was, but she did it." Carolyn leaned back in her chair. "She's a fighter. That's how come I know she'll be all right."

Rand squeezed Jessie's hand gently.

"You love her, don't you?"

He nodded.

"Saw her not too long ago. There was this glow about her. Never seen it before."

He clenched his jaw so tightly, it started to hurt. Outside the room, a door closed somewhere.

"But you're going to have to keep after her," Carolyn said a few minutes later. "She's like those horses you two vet. Proud and free. Doesn't want to be broken. Think she was broke too much in her youth. My fault, I know. But she turned out good, anyway."

When he heard the words, he realized how true they were.

"But she's a fighter," Carolyn added, her raspy voice suddenly more raspy. "She's going to wake up and you're going to marry her because my baby deserves to be happy."

SHE HEARD VOICES.

Jessie tried to focus on them, tried to hear what they were saying, but they faded as quickly as they'd come, and before she could call out, the darkness claimed her again.

Voices woke her once more. She tried to open her eyes, but couldn't. One of those voices seemed familiar. She tried to speak, but her throat hurt too much to do more than moan.

The voices stopped.

She moaned again.

But the strain of trying to wake up took too much out of her and she went back to sleep. She'd like to sleep forever….

The next time she woke up, something was different. No voices. But that whooshing noise was gone, too, she realized, thankful for that. Damn thing had driven her crazy. Her throat felt better, as well. Now if that beeping sound would just stop she'd *really* be able to get some sleep….

SHE SAW RAND the next time she regained consciousness. Actually what she saw was the top of his head. At least she thought so; it was hard to tell, her eyes were so blurry. And what was that throbbing in her skull? It felt like the world's worst hangover.

She tried to wake Rand up, but her hand wouldn't move.

That was strange. She tried again. But all she succeeded in doing was lifting a finger. Was that why her head hurt? Had she been in an accident? Was she paralyzed?

But no. She could wiggle her toes. They were far away, but she could see the sheet move. A white sheet. And a white room. Hospital.

"Rand." The word came out a croak. "Rand," she called again.

But the damn man was asleep, his head on the side of her bed.

Ah, but he held her hand.

That was good. She really wanted some water. She summoned all her strength, flexed her fingers and squeezed.

"Jessie?" Rand said softly, lifting his head.

About time.

He sat up, one side of his face creased from the sheets. Ha. Look at Dr. Rand Sheppard now.

"Jessie," he said again, his eyes meeting hers.

And then he shot up, leaning toward her, his face so filled with joy and excitement that for a moment she wondered what all the fuss was about.

"Jessie," he cried again, his eyes wide and suddenly filled with tears. "Oh, Jessie, you're awake."

Well, duh.

Chapter Twenty-Three

Rand summoned the doctor, holding on to Jessie's hand for dear life.

Awake.

She was awake. He didn't know whether to laugh or cry. Both, he decided, as he fed her some ice chips. Both.

"What happened?" she whispered.

"You don't remember?"

"Tommy?"

"He's in jail. They've charged him with assault and attempted kidnapping. That's his third strike. He's going back to jail for a long, long time."

"H-hit me?"

It took him a moment to realize she was asking if *Tommy* had hit her. Rand explained how she'd run away, then been hit by a car. A neighbor had seen the whole thing and dialed 911. The police had apprehended Tommy on his way out of town.

Jessie nodded, but the movement caused her pain. A nurse arrived then, her "Praise the Lord," echoed by Rand.

A doctor came in behind the nurse and looked Jessie over, his smile all the reassurance Rand needed.

"You should let her get some rest, though," the doctor said, glancing back at the bed. "She's going to be weak for quite some time."

When they were alone again, Rand gently brushed that errant strand of hair away from her face. "I'll be back," he murmured.

"Okay," she said.

"I love you."

She didn't answer at first, and Rand felt his heart catch. But then she smiled. "Love you, too," she whispered.

He bent forward, kissed her lightly on the nose. "Don't go anywhere."

She released a breath that he thought might be amusement. It was hard to tell.

When he got to the hall, he collapsed into a chair. She'd made it!

After they'd removed the ventilator the doctors

had told them it was up to Jessie and God whether she ever opened her eyes again. Sometimes people woke up from comas like hers, sometimes they didn't.

Jessie had woken up.

Rand didn't care that the nurse behind the counter could hear him. All his anxiety and tension was released in gut-wrenching sobs.

"Rand, what's wrong?"

He looked up. His mother stood there, Edith and Flora right behind her, fear in their faces.

"She woke up," he said, his sobs turning to laughter. "She woke up."

His mom collapsed into the chair next to him. "Oh, thank God."

JESSIE HADN'T SLEPT so much in years. Probably not since she was a baby.

And that's what she felt like: a baby. At first it was hard to move her fingers, not to mention her hands. But gradually her strength returned, until she was sitting up in bed, the cast on her leg itching like a son of a gun.

A week later she was waiting for Rand to appear. He'd taken to sneaking food into the hospital, and Jessie's mouth watered at the thought of biting into one of Frank's famous burgers. She missed the food at the diner.

"Hello, Jessie."

She stiffened; the voice was familiar...

Tommy's father.

She sank back in the bed. For a minute there he'd sounded exactly like his son.

"Is it okay if I come in?" Phil asked.

She nodded, although if she were honest with herself she wasn't certain she wanted to see him. Tommy's father had never been nice to her. But she could tell by the look on his face that he expected her to point to the door, and so she held her tongue.

"You feeling better?"

"I am," she said.

"They going to release you soon?"

"This week."

"That's good," he said. "That's good."

Mr. Lockford had aged. She'd never noticed it before.

"Look, Jessie, I wanted to tell you how sorry I am."

His eyes were a lot like Tommy's. That made her shiver.

"There's no excusing my son's behavior, I know. But I offer you an apology."

"Apology accepted," she said.

He nodded, yet he still didn't leave. He'd come here to say something else, although she couldn't begin to fathom what.

"I wronged you in the past. When someone you love does something you can't believe, it's easy to look elsewhere for the blame. I didn't want Tommy to be guilty of those crimes, so I looked for a scapegoat." His eyes never wavered. "I found you."

"It's okay," she said. "I understand."

"No, I don't think you do," he said. "I caught Tommy with some other stuff. Not drugs. Just things that I realize now he must have stolen. At the time he told me they were given to him, but after he went off to jail I started asking around."

She didn't really understand where this was going.

"I knew he'd lied to me back then."

Jessie heard footsteps. A nurse poked her head in. Jessie gave her the thumbs-up, and she went back out.

"I should have confronted him when he got out of prison, but I was so damn glad to have him back. I wanted to believe…" He leaned forward, and for a second Jessie thought he might clasp her hand. "I wanted to believe the past was behind us. But then Rand came by after you two had been to the rodeo, and I realized that Tommy wasn't the boy I thought I'd raised."

She sat up suddenly, the movement causing her leg to twinge. She ignored it. "After the rodeo?"

Phil nodded. "He came to see me the night you returned. Asked me to tell Tommy that if he ever touched you again, he'd kill him."

"What?"

"You didn't know he'd come by?"

As far as she'd known, Rand had only visited his uncle after he'd overheard Tommy's confession. But if he'd gone to him before, that meant...

Oh, jeez. Rand had believed in her *before* Tommy's confession.

"I didn't know," she said.

"Well, he did. But I ignored him, thought you'd turned his head with pretty words and...other things." Phil looked embarrassed, ashamed. "I should have talked to my son then, but I didn't. I didn't believe Rand until his second visit when he confronted Tommy in front of me and I could see the look in my son's eyes. I knew I'd made a horrible mistake."

"It's okay," Jessie said, smiling. "Really. I know

what it's like when someone you love lets you down."

"You do?"

She nodded. "My dad. I used to think the sun rose and set on him. He used to pick me up and swing me around, you know, like you're a human carnival ride or something. I was five years old when he left us, and I still remember the hurt I felt when I realized he wasn't coming back."

"I'm sure you do," he said, his shoulders slumped. A nurse walked by outside, and they both looked up for a moment.

"It was like that with my mom's second husband, too. Here today, gone tomorrow," Jessie said into the silence.

She felt the breath leave her as realization dawned.

And maybe it was fate, or the hand of God, but Rand walked into her room at that moment, a wide smile on his face, holding a white foam carton with her contraband hamburger behind a giant vase of flowers.

"Phil," he said, stopping near the foot of her bed.

"Hello, Rand. I was just leaving. Come on in."

Rand looked from one to the other. Jessie gave him a reassuring smile. "Bye, Phil," she said softly.

"Take care, Jessie," he said.

She held out a hand to the older man. He took it, surprised. "Thanks for coming by," she said.

He seemed close to tears. She saw his throat work, his jaw tight. "Thanks for having me."

He let her go, clapping Rand on the shoulder on the way by. "You got yourself a good one there, son."

Rand didn't say a word as he set the flowers down, the smells of roses and hamburgers something Jessie would forever associate with that moment.

"What was that all about?" he asked, taking the seat his uncle had vacated.

"Why didn't you tell me you went to see Phil after the rodeo?"

"I *did* tell you."

"No, you told me you were going to see Tommy."

Rand set the carton down next to her. Jessie ignored it even though her stomach grumbled in protest.

"I didn't think you needed to know."

"Why not?"

"Because you were mad at me. And to be honest, the next day I overheard Tommy in the barn, and so it seemed immaterial. The truth came out in another way. Besides, I had a feeling you wouldn't believe me if I told you. You have an annoying habit of thinking the worst of me."

"I know." The revelation she'd had a moment before shed new light on her behavior toward Rand. "I know," she repeated softly, shaking her head.

"You want to eat?" he asked, holding up the box.

"No, I want to say I'm sorry."

"For what?"

"For being such an idiot. I have an annoying habit of believing the worst about *everyone,* not just you. I thought the whole town hated me until you brought me to that charity auction. I thought your mom and your family wouldn't think I was good enough. But worst of all, I didn't trust you enough to believe that you'd want to stay with me."

"What?"

She nodded. "That's why I gave you your ring back. The thing that frightened me the most was that one day you'd up and leave me."

"Jessie, I'd never do that."

"I know," she said. "You stood by my bedside even when you thought I might not make it. You held my hand knowing I might wake up and never walk. Or speak. That I might have some kind of brain damage, which, when you think about it, I obviously already had."

"Oh, Jessie."

"I'm sorry, Rand," she said. "So sorry for being such a pain—"

"Shh," he soothed, bending forward and kissing her on the lips. "It's done. You're here with me now."

"No," she said, cupping his cheek with her hand. "What's important is that I tell you how much I love you. How much I want to be with you. Now. For always. Forever."

"Jessie," he said. "Sweet Jessie. From the day I met you, you've been a challenge. You didn't honestly think I would throw in the towel so easily?"

"I did."

"And now?"

"I realize I'm the luckiest woman in the world."

"Just as long as you keep remembering that," he said, before kissing her.

"Well, well, well," said someone from the door. "What have we here?"

Jessie giggled when she saw Martha standing near the door.

Rand looked at Jessie. "Two people in love, Mom. Just two people in love."

Epilogue

"I'm going to beat you," Jessie called to Rand, her laughter trailing back to him over the sound of his horse's pounding hooves.

"Oh, no, you're not," he said, spurring his gelding forward.

She laughed again as the two of them thundered up the trail. Closer and closer he edged, but the horse she rode was one of the fastest on the ranch, and Jessie's cry was filled with glee when she made it to the summit first.

"I won!" She raised one hand in victory, using the other to pull her horse to a stop. "Ha ha! I kicked your butt."

Rand pulled his horse up right next to her, a smile on his face even though, as she so rudely noted, she'd kicked his butt.

She could kick his butt any day.

It'd been six months since her stay in the hospital. Six months since that tearful day when she'd finally realized he loved her, and that he wasn't going anywhere. Six months of painful recovery here at the ranch, where his mother had insisted she stay.

"Hey," Jessie said, looking around. "How'd we end up here?"

He smiled. "There's more than one path up to this summit."

"I didn't even realize we were near this place."

It was the same plateau he'd brought her to all those months ago, the place where he'd asked her to marry him.

"Of course you didn't," he said. "I didn't want you to know."

"Didn't want me to—"

Her eyes widened as realization dawned. "Oh, Rand."

He got off his horse. She stayed mounted, love and tenderness in her expression as she watched.

"Rand asks Jessie to marry him, take two," he said.

She covered her mouth with her hands. Her horse took a step, but she expertly maintained control.

"I know we've had our ups and downs. I know we tried once before, but I'm hoping we can start again." He got down on one knee. "Jessie, will you marry me?"

And this time there was no fear in her eyes as she slowly climbed down from her horse. This time her voice didn't waver as she said yes.

And when she held out her hand, it didn't shake as he slid on the ring.

"Yes," she said again, slipping into his arms.

Rand closed his eyes, holding her. Nothing could be more perfect than having her in his arms.

"I love you," she said softly.

"I love you, too," he said. "And if you want to go to vet school, that's fine. And if you don't want kids, that's fine, too. Waiting for you to wake up in that damn hospital, I realized nothing mattered except being with you."

"I know." When she drew back, he saw the truth in her eyes. "I know."

"And I'm not going any place, either, Jessie Munroe, so you can get that idea right out of your head."

She smiled crookedly. "You better not, Rand Sheppard, or I'll hunt you down and sick Flora, Edith and your mother on you."

He shivered theatrically. She laughed.

And then they kissed.

The sun began to set around them, but Jessie and Rand didn't notice. They were too wrapped up in the joy of being in each other's arms, a joy that would be with them each and every day of their lives. And their children's lives.

* * * * *

Ambience is everything. Imagine eating a foie gras at a luncheonette counter, or a side of cole slaw at Le Cirque. It's not a matter of food but one of atmosphere. Remember that when planning your dining room design.
—Tips from *Teddi.com*

"Now that's the kind of man you should be looking for," my mother, the self-appointed keeper of my shelf-life stamp, says. She points with her fork at a man in the corner of the Steak-Out Restaurant, a dive I've just been hired to redecorate. Making this restaurant look four-star will be hard, but not half as hard as getting through lunch without strangling the woman across the table from me. "*He* would make a good husband."

"Oh, you can tell that from across the room?" I ask, wondering how it is she can forget that when we had trouble getting rid of my last husband, she shot him. "Besides being ten minutes away from death if he actually eats all that steak, he's twenty years too old for me and—shallow woman that I am—twenty pounds too heavy. Besides, I am *so* not looking for another husband here. I'm looking to design a new image for this place, looking for some sense of ambience, some feeling, something I can build a proposal on for them."

My mother studies the man in the corner, tilting her head, the better to gauge his age, I suppose. I think she's grimacing, but with all the Botox and Restylane injected into that face, it's hard to tell. She takes another bite of her steak salad, chews slowly so that I don't miss the fact that the steak is a poor cut and tougher than it should be. "You're concentrating on the wrong kind of proposal," she says finally. "Just look at this place, Teddi. It's a dive. There are hardly any other diners. What does *that* tell you about the food?"

"That they cater to a dinner crowd and it's lunchtime," I tell her.

I don't know what I was thinking bringing her here with me. I suppose I thought it would be better than eating alone. There really are days when my common sense goes on vacation. Clearly, this is one of them. I mean, really, did I not resolve less than three weeks ago that I would not let my mother get to me anymore?

What good are New Year's resolutions, anyway?

Mario approaches the man's table and my mother studies him while they converse. Eventually Mario leaves the table with a huff, after which the diner glances up and meets my mother's gaze. I think she's smiling at him. That or she's got indigestion. They size each other up.

I concentrate on making sketches in my notebook and try to ignore the fact that my mother is flirting. At nearly seventy, she's developed an unhealthy interest in members of the opposite sex to whom she isn't married.

According to my father, who has broken the TMI rule and given me Too Much Information, she has no interest in sex with him. Better, I suppose, to be clued in on what they aren't doing in the bedroom than have to hear what they might be doing.

"He's not so old," my mother says, noticing that I have barely touched the Chinese chicken salad she warned me not to get. "He's got about as many years on you as you have on your little cop friend."

She does this to make me crazy. I know it, but it works all the same. "Drew Scoones is not my little 'friend.' He's a detective with whom I—"

"Screwed around," my mother says. I must look shocked, because my mother laughs at me and asks if I think she doesn't know the "lingo."

What I thought she didn't know was that Drew and I actually tangled in the sheets. And, since it's possible she's just fishing, I sidestep the issue and tell her that Drew is just a couple of years younger than me and that I don't need reminding. I dig into my salad with renewed vigor, determined to show my mother that Chinese chicken salad in a steak place was not the stupid choice it's proving to be.

After a few more minutes of my picking at the wilted leaves on my plate, the man my mother has me nearly engaged to pays his bill and heads past us toward the back of the restaurant. I watch my mother take in his shoes, his suit and the diamond pinkie ring that seems to be cutting off the circulation in his little finger.

"Such nice hands," she says after the man is out

of sight. "Manicured." She and I both stare at my hands. I have two popped acrylics that are being held on at weird angles by bandages. My cuticles are ragged and there's marker decorating my right hand from measuring carelessly when I did a drawing for a customer.

Twenty minutes later she's disappointed that he managed to leave the restaurant without our noticing. He will join the list of the ones I let get away. I will hear about him twenty years from now when—according to my mother—my children will be grown and I will still be single, living pathetically alone with several dogs and cats.

After my ex, that sounds good to me.

The waitress tells us that our meal has been taken care of by the management and, after thanking Mario, the owner, complimenting him on the wonderful meal and assuring him that once I have redecorated his place people will be flocking here in droves (I actually use those words and ignore my mother when she rolls her eyes), my mother and I head for the restroom.

My father—unfortunately not with us today— has the patience of a saint. He got it over the years of living with my mother. She, perhaps as a result, figures he has the patience for both of them, and feels justified having none. For her, no rules apply, and a little thing like a picture of a man on the door to a public restroom is certainly no barrier to using the john. In all fairness, it does seem silly to stand and wait for the ladies' room if no one is using the men's room.

Still, it's the idea that rules don't apply to her, signs don't apply to her, conventions don't apply to her. She knocks on the door to the men's room. When no one answers she gestures to me to go in ahead. I tell her that I can certainly wait for the ladies' room to be free and she shrugs and goes in herself.

Not a minute later there is a bloodcurdling scream from behind the men's room door.

"Mom!" I yell. "Are you all right?"

Mario comes running over, the waitress on his heels. Two customers head our way while my mother continues to scream.

I try the door, but it is locked. I yell for her to open it and she fumbles with the knob. When she finally manages to unlock and open it, she is white behind her two streaks of blush, but she is on her feet and appears shaken but not stirred.

"What happened?" I ask her. So do Mario and

the waitress and the few customers who have migrated to the back of the place.

She points toward the bathroom and I go in, thinking it serves her right for using the men's room. But I see nothing amiss.

She gestures toward the stall, and, like any self-respecting and suspicious woman, I poke the door open with one finger, expecting the worst.

What I find is worse than the worst.

The husband my mother picked out for me is sitting on the toilet. His pants are puddled around his ankles, his hands are hanging at his sides. Pinned to his chest is some sort of Health Department certificate.

Oh, and there is a large, round, bloodless bullet hole between his eyes.

Four Nassau County police officers are securing the area, waiting for the detectives and crime scene personnel to show up. They are trying, though not very hard, to comfort my mother, who in another era would be considered to be suffering from the vapors. Less tactful in the twenty-first century, I'd say she was losing it. That is, if I didn't know her better, know she was milking it for everything it was worth.

My mother loves attention. As it begins to flag,

she swoons and claims to feel faint. Despite four No Smoking signs, my mother insists it's all right for her to light up because, after all, she's in shock. Not to mention that signs, as we know, don't apply to her.

When asked not to smoke, she collapses mournfully in a chair and lets her head loll to the side, all without mussing her hair.

Eventually, the detectives show up to find the four patrolmen all circled around her, debating whether to administer CPR, smelling salts or simply call the paramedics. I, however, know just what will snap her to attention.

"Detective Scoones," I say loudly. My mother parts the sea of cops.

"We have to stop meeting like this," he says lightly to me, but I can feel him checking me over with his eyes, making sure I'm all right while pretending not to care.

"What have you got in those pants?" my mother asks him, coming to her feet and staring at his crotch accusingly. "*Baydar?* Everywhere we Bayers are, you turn up. You don't expect me to buy that this is a coincidence, I hope."

Drew tells my mother that it's nice to see her, too, and asks if it's his fault that her daughter seems to attract disasters.

Charming to be made to feel like the bearer of a plague.

He asks how I am.

"Just peachy," I tell him. "I seem to be making a habit of finding dead bodies, my mother is driving me crazy and the catering hall I booked two freakin' years ago for Dana's bat mitzvah has just been shut down by the Board of Health!"

"Glad to see your luck's finally changing," he says, giving me a quick squeeze around the shoulders before turning his attention to the patrolmen, asking what they've got, whether they've taken any statements, moved anything, all the sort of stuff you see on TV, without any of the drama. That is, if you don't count my mother's threats to faint every few minutes when she senses no one's paying attention to her.

Mario tells his waitstaff to bring everyone espresso, which I decline because I'm wired enough. Drew pulls him aside and a minute later I'm handed a cup of coffee that smells divinely of Kahlúa.

The man knows me well. Too well.

His partner, whom I've met once or twice, says he'll interview the kitchen staff. Drew asks Mario if he minds if he takes statements from the patrons first and gets to him and the wait staff afterward.

"No, no," Mario tells him. "Do the patrons first." Drew raises his eyebrow at me like he wants to know if I get the double entendre. I try to look bored.

"What is it with you and murder victims?" he asks me when we sit down at a table in the corner.

I search them out so that I can see you again, I almost say, but I'm afraid it will sound desperate instead of sarcastic.

My mother, lighting up and daring him with a look to tell her not to, reminds him that *she* was the one to find the body.

Drew asks what happened *this time*. My mother tells him how the man in the john was "taken" with me, couldn't take his eyes off me and blatantly flirted with both of us. To his credit, Drew doesn't laugh, but his smirk is undeniable to the trained eye. And I've had my eye trained on him for nearly a year now.

"While he was noticing you," he asks me, "did *you* notice anything about him? Was he waiting for anyone? Watching for anything?"

I tell him that he didn't appear to be waiting or watching. That he made no phone calls, was fairly intent on eating and did, indeed, flirt with my mother. This last bit Drew takes with a grain of salt, which was the way it was intended.

"And he had a short conversation with Mario," I tell him. "I think he might have been unhappy with the food, though he didn't send it back."

Drew asks what makes me think he was dissatisfied, and I tell him that the discussion seemed acrimonious and that Mario looked distressed when he left the table. Drew makes a note and says he'll look into it and asks about anyone else in the restaurant. Did I see anyone who didn't seem to belong, anyone who was watching the victim, anyone looking suspicious?

"Besides my mother?" I ask him, and Mom huffs and blows her cigarette smoke in my direction.

I tell him that there were several deliveries, the kitchen staff going in and out the back door to grab a smoke. He stops me and asks what I was doing checking out the back door of the restaurant.

Proudly—because, while he was off forgetting me, dropping by only once in a while to say hi to Jesse, my son, or drop something by for one of my daughters that he thought they might like, I was getting on with my life—I tell him that I'm decorating the place.

He looks genuinely impressed. "Commercial

customers? That's great," he says. Okay, that's what he *ought* to say. What he actually says is "Whatever pays the bills."

"Howard Rosen, the famous restaurant critic, got her the job," my mother says. "You met him— the good-looking, distinguished gentleman with the *real* job, something to be proud of. I guess you've never read his reviews in *Newsday*."

Drew, without missing a beat, tells her that Howard's reviews are on the top of his list, as soon as he learns how to read.

"I only meant—" my mother starts, but both of us assure her that we know just what she meant.

"So," Drew says. "Deliveries?"

I tell him that Mario would know better than I, but that I saw vegetables come in, maybe fish and linens.

"This is the second restaurant job Howard's got her," my mother tells Drew.

"At least she's getting *something* out of the relationship," he says.

"If he were here," my mother says, ignoring the insinuation, "he'd be comforting her instead of interrogating her. He'd be making sure we're both all right after such an ordeal."

"I'm sure he would," Drew agrees, then looks me

in the eyes as if he's measuring my tolerance for shock. Quietly he adds, "But then maybe he doesn't know just what strong stuff your daughter's made of."

It's the closest thing to a tender moment I can expect from Drew Scoones. My mother breaks the spell. "She gets that from me," she says.

Both Drew and I take a minute, probably to pray that's all I inherited from her.

"I'm just trying to save you some time and effort," my mother tells him. "My money's on Howard."

Drew withers her with a look and mutters something that sounds suspiciously like "fool's gold." Then he excuses himself to go back to work.

I catch his sleeve and ask if it's all right for us to leave. He says sure, he knows where we live. I say goodbye to Mario. I assure him that I will have some sketches for him in a few days, all the while hoping that this murder doesn't cancel his redecorating plans. I need the money desperately, the alternative being borrowing from my parents and being strangled by the strings.

My mother is strangely quiet all the way to her house. She doesn't tell me what a loser Drew Scoones is—despite his good looks—and how I was obviously drooling over him. She doesn't ask me where Howard is taking me tonight or warn me not to tell my father about what happened because he will worry about us both and no doubt insist we see our respective psychiatrists.

She fidgets nervously, opening and closing her purse over and over again.

"You okay?" I ask her. After all, she's just found a dead man on the toilet, and tough as she is that's got to be upsetting.

When she doesn't answer me I pull over to the side of the road.

"Mom?" She refuses to meet my eyes. "You want me to take you to see Dr. Cohen?"

She looks out the window as if she's just realized we're on Broadway in Woodmere. "Aren't we near Marvin's Jewelers?" she asks, pulling something out of her purse.

"What have you got, Mother?" I ask, prying open her fingers to find the murdered man's ring.

"It was on the sink," she says in answer to my dropped jaw. "I was going to get his name and address and have you return it to him so that he could ask you out. I thought it was a sign that the two of you were meant to be together."

"He's dead, Mom. You understand that, right?" I ask. You never can tell when my mother is fine and when she's in la-la land.

"Well, I didn't know that," she shouts at me. "Not at the time."

I ask why she didn't give it to Drew, realize that she wouldn't give Drew the time in a clock shop and add, "…or one of the other policemen?"

"For heaven's sake," she tells me. "The man is dead, Teddi, and I took his ring. How would that look?"

Before I can tell her it looks just the way it is, she pulls out a cigarette and threatens to light it.

"I mean, really," she says, shaking her head like it's my brains that are loose. "What does he need with it now?"

Silhouette®

nocturne™

**WAS HE HER SAVIOR
OR HER NIGHTMARE?**

HAUNTED
LISA CHILDS

Years ago, Ariel and her sisters were separated for
their own protection. Now the man who vowed
revenge on her family has resumed the hunt, and
Ariel must warn her sisters before it's too late.
The closer she comes to finding them, the more
secretive her fiancé becomes. Can she trust the man
she plans to spend eternity with? Or has he been
waiting for the perfect moment to destroy her?

On sale December 2006.

REQUEST YOUR FREE BOOKS!
2 FREE NOVELS PLUS 2
FREE GIFTS!

Heart, Home & Happiness!

In February, expect MORE
from

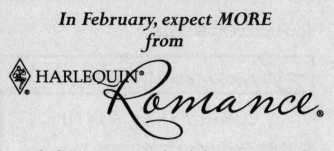

as it increases to six titles per month.

What's to come...

Rancher and Protector

Part of the
Western Weddings
miniseries

BY JUDY CHRISTENBERRY

The Boss's Pregnancy Proposal

BY RAYE MORGAN

Don't miss February's
incredible line up of authors!

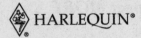

HARLEQUIN®

American ROMANCE®

COMING NEXT MONTH

#1145 DADDY NEXT DOOR by Judy Christenberry
Dallas Duets

Nick Barry thought his new Dallas apartment was the perfect place to launch his career…until he was bowled over by the trio of towheaded children next door—and their gorgeous new mommy, Jennifer Carpenter. She had no time for a man; besides, the hunk across the hall wouldn't want a ready-made family. Too bad he was downright irresistible!

#1146 THE FAMILY RESCUE by Kara Lennox
Firehouse 59

After rookie firefighter Ethan Basque rescues Kathryn Holiday and her seven-year-old daughter from a fire that burned down their home, he can't get them out of his mind. He offers them a place to stay—but can Ethan convince Kat he's not just trying to be a hero, and will he be there for her always?

#1147 HER MILITARY MAN by Laura Marie Altom

Constance Price, aka Miss Manners, is at her wit's end when her boss wants Garret Underwood, her biggest critic and the man she once loved, on her radio program. Thankfully the navy SEAL is in town only temporarily. Maybe Connie can save her show…and still keep their ten-year-old daughter's existence a secret.

#1148 NELSON IN COMMAND by Marin Thomas
The McKade Brothers

Nelson McKade was a CEO—until his grandfather sent him to learn humility at a dairy farm set to go "udders up." The power broker decided to play along with farm owner Ellen Tanner's plan to save the day. But he also had a few *un*businesslike moves in mind to get the gorgeous widow to see things *his* way.

www.eHarlequin.com